"Enjoying your holiday?" Mike asked casually.

"Yes, very much so."

"Been here long?"

"We've only just arrived." Catherine smiled rather shyly.

"Renting the place?" Mike continued in that same casual tone.

"Oh no," Catherine breathed. "We're guests."

Mike's black brows rose dramatically over the midnight blue of his eyes. He supposed "guests" was one way of putting it! "And who invited you?"

"Mr. Donahue," she stated almost proudly.

"You're lying!" Mike snarled. "I'm Donahue!"

Rosemary Badger was born in Montreal, Canada, and when she was seventeen she attended a college football match, took one look at a tall, dark, handsome player and confided to her best friend, "I'm going to marry that man."

And two years later—she did!

Rosemary decided she wanted to write for Harlequin when she turned forty and her first book was published in 1983. She and her husband now live in tropical Queensland, Australia, with their four children. They love to swim, sail and spend as many weekends as they can at their small bush property at Apple Tree Creek.

Books by Rosemary Badger

HARLEQUIN ROMANCE
165—DANCING WITH SHADOWS
2773—SHADOWS OF EDEN
2827—TIME TO TRUST
2864—THE GOOD-TIME GUY

SWEET DESIRE
Rosemary Badger

Harlequin Books

TORONTO • NEW YORK • LONDON
AMSTERDAM • PARIS • SYDNEY • HAMBURG
STOCKHOLM • ATHENS • TOKYO • MILAN
MADRID • WARSAW • BUDAPEST • AUCKLAND

ISBN 0-373-17228-1

SWEET DESIRE

CHAPTER ONE

THE little red MG flew past the fields of gently swaying green sugar-cane, the purple flowering tops announcing time for harvest. The air was thick with the sweet scent of sugar as plantation owners torched their crops to rid it of weeds, leaves and other pests before harvesting. Straight ahead was the village clock, and beyond it lay the sparkling blue waters of the mighty Pacific on Australia's sub-tropical eastern coast. Twenty-eight-year-old Catherine Mitchell glanced down at her seven-year-old daughter and grinned. Jessie looked every inch the tourist with her brand new sunglasses perched on the bridge of her nose and her equally new camera slung around her neck.

'Grandma said to make a right turn at the clock,' Catherine told her as she swung the ancient MG in that direction. The sea breeze tossed her shoulder-length mane of thick reddish chestnut-coloured hair about her face and she raised a slender hand to push it back. They had made the four-hour trip north to Bargara from Brisbane with the top down and Catherine was beginning to feel the effects of being totally windblown.

'How much further now, Mummy?' Jessie asked impatiently as she tugged at a reddish brown curl poking rather jauntily from beneath the straw brim of her hat.

'According to Grandma, five kilometres from the clock. The Donahue mansion is the last house on the left and our little cottage tucked away beyond it. It won't be long now, my impatient little poppet,' Catherine smiled as she pulled up to a stop sign and adjusted her rear-view mirror to check the damage done to her hair.

A horn blared behind them. Startled, Catherine caught sight of a dark-haired man wearing sunglasses in her rear-view mirror. He waved an impatient hand at her from behind the wheel of a very impressive silver grey Jaguar convertible. An indignant flush swept over her cheeks as she moved across the inter-section. The man obviously thought she was ad-miring herself in the mirror while holding up the traffic. She gave him a withering glare which he totally ignored as he roared past them and disappeared around a corner.

The magnificent waterfront homes lined the fore-shore and Catherine felt her excitement growing. This was her and Jessie's first ever holiday. Life had been a struggle since the drowning of her young husband when Jessie was barely three. Stunned with grief and with no money behind her, Catherine had worked at whatever jobs she could find while still managing to put herself through university, knowing that, if she wanted to provide a decent future for her child, she had to equip herself with a degree. Two weeks ago she had graduated and would start her first teaching position at a high school in Bundaberg, a mere twelve kilometres from Bargara.

The last house on the left appeared and Catherine stopped the car at the driveway entrance. Her mother had claimed the house was a gracious mansion and she had been right.

'This is it!' Catherine breathed as her beautiful hazel eyes fell on a handsome brass plaque with the name 'DONAHUE' spelt out in bold black letters. Jessie unbuckled her seatbelt and perched her little bottom on top of the back of her seat to get a better view.

Palm trees lined the pink cobbled driveway leading up to the white double storeyed giant. Gleaming white pillars supported the upper storey and tall, wide windows would provide spectacular views of the sweeping surf. French doors opened on to the wide verandas and the whole structure was trimmed with delicate white lace ironwork, adding even more elegance to the beautiful home. Thick green lawns broken with ornamental shrubs completed the picture.

The mansion belonged to Mike Donahue, the tough thirty-six-year-old employer of her mother. Three months ago, Mike's father had suffered a stroke. Catherine's mother, Betty White, had nursed him in hospital. Albert had become dependent on her, refusing attentions from any other nurse and becoming highly agitated whenever Betty was off duty. When it came time for Albert to be discharged from hospital, doctors recommended a nursing home. Mike had refused to even consider such an option and had approached Catherine's mother to nurse his father privately at his seaside home at Bargara. Widowed herself at an early age, Betty had been more than happy to finally say goodbye to the demanding rigours of a hospital ward for the easier and more rewarding job of getting Albert on his feet again. Besides, she had become rather fond of the sage old character.

And it had been this same sage character who had so thoughtfully invited Catherine and Jessie to spend

the long Christmas vacation at the small cottage on
his son's estate which was 'going to waste'. Betty had
driven her old blue Ford down to Brisbane for
Catherine's graduation. She had handed Catherine a
gift and a note, both from Albert. The gift was an
exquisite gold watch and the note an invitation to
spend the summer at Bargara. Deeply touched and
filled with gratitude, Catherine had sent a note back,
thanking Albert for his beautiful gift and his wonderful invitation. She naturally assumed the invitation came with his son's blessing.

It occurred to Catherine, as she sat dreamily gazing
up at the spectacular mansion, that although she had
never met either Albert or his son, there wasn't much
she didn't know about them. During their months
together, Albert had filled Betty's ears with glowing
accounts of his son. Betty had passed this information on to her daughter and Catherine assumed
Mike had heard the odd tit-bit about herself as well.
After all, it was only natural for parents to discuss
their offspring with any interested party. She knew,
for instance, that Mike had taken over the reins of
the moderately successful Donahue Corporation ten
years ago when Albert had retired due to failing
health. Mike had diversified and expanded their operations into the four corners of the world. His brilliant engineering skills and uncanny knack for
knowing what would succeed had led the young
entrepreneur into mining, logging, oil drilling and
property development. The Donahue Corporation was
now one of the most successful and powerful cor-
porations in the world. She also knew Mike was di-
vorced, that his wife had remarried and their nine-
year-old daughter, Lucy, was visiting her mother in

Texas. She had been told Mike was presently in Borneo, wrapping up the final stage of his newly constructed steel plant. He was expected home by the end of summer and Catherine hoped to meet him then. It would be wonderful to hear about all the lands he had worked in; places she could only dream about without ever expecting to see.

'Are we going to go up and say hello to Grandma?' Jessie wanted to know.

'No, darling. Grandma will be over later after we've had a chance to settle in at the cottage.'

As she spoke Catherine's eyes were drawn suddenly to an upstairs window. A curtain had been pulled partly back and they were being watched by a woman. Even through the fair distance separating them, Catherine could feel this woman's hostility. She rather suspected the tall, imposing figure belonged to Mrs Beasley, Mike Donahue's housekeeper who kept his domestic affairs in order while he was away. Despite Betty's attempts to be friendly with her, Mrs Beasley had refused any overtures. Her mother had confided to Catherine that she rather suspected poor Mrs Beasley thought she was after her job.

Feeling oddly uneasy, Catherine started the motor of her vehicle and ordered Jessie to do up her seatbelt. As she pulled away from the driveway, the silver-grey Jaguar rounded the bend and sped towards them, adding to her sense of unease. She accelerated and the red MG shot forward.

Mike Donahue frowned. He had recognised the vehicle and its windswept driver and wondered what had prompted her to park in front of his driveway. Well, she certainly wouldn't get far. The no through road ended just past Dune Cottage, the small original homestead on his estate. As he swung the Jag on to the pink cobbled driveway he noticed the figure at the window and his frown deepened. Mrs Beasley didn't appear particularly happy. He wondered what further mischief Lucy had been up to since her arrival home from Texas.

In fact it was on Lucy's account that Mike had made it home much earlier than he had planned. The child had managed to weave her way through a battery of international operators to reach him at his quarters in Borneo. She had been upset, her tearful little voice claiming she was homesick, and had begged to come home. Mike had made the necessary flight arrangements himself, not trusting Gail, his ex-wife, to carry out such a responsibility. Lucy had been home for a few days now and during that brief time Mrs Beasley had rung him several times, distressed about the child's behaviour. She had broken a window, tipped over every vase of flowers in the entire house and refused to go to bed before midnight. She had hidden her grandfather's medication and carved her initials in his cane. While Mike realised the child's behaviour was probably due to not receiving the loving attention she had hoped for from her mother, she had to be brought back into line and harmony restored to his household. He would manage this in the short time he planned to be home.

As he strode towards the house, it occurred to him he hadn't seen nor heard the red MG returning from the no through road. He lifted his powerful shoulders in a shrug. He had more important things to occupy his mind than wondering what had become of the wind-blown brunette and her battered little sports car.

*　　*　　*

Catherine found the key just where her mother had promised it would be: under a flowerpot on the back kitchen step. She and Jessie fell in love with the small white cottage as soon as they opened the door. There were four tiny rooms, the kitchen and lounge separated from the two bedrooms by a short, narrow hall. At the far end of the hall was a bathroom-cum-laundry. Every room in the house had a beautiful view of the ocean and, when they had opened all the windows, the cottage was filled with a refreshing sea breeze. It didn't take long to unload the car and store away their belongings. Catherine had brought along a few supplies to keep them going until they went shopping in the village, but when she opened the cupboards and fridge she found them already well stocked. There was even a bottle of white wine.

They had their evening meal on the front veranda facing the ocean. The cottage was totally isolated, hidden from the world by majestic sand dunes and a young forest of trees on their left and a deeper, wilder wood to their right. Catherine knew via her mother's letters that Mike had planted the young forest separating the mansion from the cottage. Coral-coloured hibiscus shrubs in need of a good pruning hugged the walls of the cottage, and the grass surrounding it was overgrown. But none of this detracted from the cottage. Catherine had never felt happier or more at peace. It's the salt air, she thought. That and knowing I have a job I can be proud of, a steady means of support for my baby girl. She smiled at Jessie and Jessie beamed back.

'Look, Mummy!' she exclaimed, and pointed. 'Our little cottage has its own name!'

Catherine looked where Jessie pointed. Beside the door, nailed to the white chamferboard, was a wooden plaque with the words 'Dune Cottage' clearly spelt out. It only added to Catherine's joy. The cottage became even more special.

When the shadows lengthened and the ocean deepened in colour it became apparent that Betty wasn't going to make it over that evening. Catherine tucked Jessie into bed and left her to dream in her pretty little bedroom with its white cane furnishings. Catherine took a refreshing shower and slipped into a long white cotton nightie. With a glass of the chilled white wine in her hand she went out to sit on the veranda to gaze dreamily at the flickering stars and watch the moon splash its beams across the velvet black of the ocean. The sand dunes rose like majestic silver castles under the pale moonlight. Catherine placed her glass on the rounded white cane table and stepped barefoot on to the soft, powdery sand.

She wanted to climb the dunes. She was possessed with an irresistible urge to climb to the top, lift her arms to the moon, shout her joy to the heavens and capture a star in her outstretched hand. She felt she would burst if she didn't!

Mike leaned against the smooth white pillar on the tiled veranda of his home. It was ten o'clock and all was finally quiet in his household. He leaned there, hands thrust deeply into the pockets of his black trousers, the sleeves of his white shirt rolled up his forearms and his feet crossed at the ankles.

The night was perfect, the sea breeze soft and balmy. It lifted the straight black hair from his wide, intelligent brow and made his scalp feel good. His newly constructed steel plant had been built without any major problems. He had left his men in Borneo to tie up any loose ends. Not that he expected any, but it would give his crews a chance to unwind before they packed and started the journey home.

Mike turned his mind to his next project, a massive ski resort in British Columbia. And the thrill he used to experience when embarking on something new and adventurous didn't come. The sea pounded in front of him, filling him with a brooding restlessness. He was home for a few weeks. Perhaps by the end of it he wouldn't feel so... distanced from himself. And he needed to spend time with Lucy, plan for her future schooling. The child was obviously becoming too much for Beasley to handle, and boarding school seemed the only alternative.

He thought of their behaviour tonight and frowned. Lucy had complained and fidgeted the whole evening until he had finally ordered her to bed. Nurse Betty White appeared anxious, nervously glancing at her watch every few minutes as though she was being kept from a very important appointment. Beasley had seemed smug, secretive somehow, looking very much like a cat who had swallowed the mouse every time she had glanced at Nurse. While his father looked better than he had for some time, he too seemed at odds, bemused by the two women. Something was up. He shifted his position to gaze down at the sand dunes jutting majestically into the midnight black of the skies.

The dunes were an unique landmark and one of the reasons he had purchased this vast estate comprising of two hundred hectares of absolute waterfront. There was a natural cove in front of Dune Cottage which would make an excellent marina for the resort he would build after his project in British Columbia was completed. He had already subdivided the land, keeping fifty hectares for the house and the remainder for the resort. Trees had been planted and growing well. They would serve as a natural buffer between his home and resort.

There was movement on the dunes. Mike's eyes narrowed as his body became instantly alert. A woman stood at the edge of the dunes, dressed entirely in white. Her dark hair was lifted in the soft breeze and swirled about her shoulders. She stood still and the same breeze which played with her hair tugged at her skirt, moulding it to the feminine curve of her hip and thigh. Suddenly she started to sway as though listening to some inner beat. Intrigued, Mike continued to watch, unable to tear his eyes from the beautiful vision she made.

She swayed faster and faster and her hair swirled about her head like a shimmering dark cloud. Suddenly she reached down, picked up the hem of her long gown and inched it slowly, seductively up her body, her swaying movements continuing as she pulled it over her head and released it from her fingers. The garment floated in the whispery breeze before fluttering down to her feet. She stood under the soft moonlight, her lovely naked body silhouetted against the darkened sky.

Slowly she raised her arms, high above her head, her outstretched fingers pretending to pluck the stars from their heavenly bed. She pressed them to her lips and blew them back and then she embraced the sky and the moon. She ran lightly across the dunes and then returned to stand at the edge. For several moments she stood quite still, then picked up the rhythmic beat of her sway. Mike felt heat spread swiftly in his loins. The girl picked up her nightie but she didn't put it on. She allowed it to trail behind her as she danced in total abandonment across the dunes. As suddenly as she had appeared, she was gone and it was like she had never been there at all so brief was her visit.

Mike let out his breath in a long lingering sigh, not even aware that he had been holding it back. For a moment, a rare brief moment, he had felt her joy, her total abandonment, her zest for living. And it had felt good.

He pushed himself away from the pillar, down the wide broad steps and on to the beach. He had to find this rare, wild creature even if just to convince himself she hadn't been a figment of his imagination. He had been fifty-six hours without sleep, having stopped several times to check on other business developments on his way back from Borneo, and he knew he was exhausted. Perhaps he had been dreaming. But if she was real, did exist outside his imagination, then he was determined to find out what she was doing trespassing on his property and, of all things, dancing naked on his dunes!

'Daddy?'

The young voice caught him and turned him around. Lucy stood in the doorway, her long blonde hair dishevelled and her usually cross little face now softened with the lingering traces of sleep.

'What is it, Lucy?' he asked gently, tenderness swelling his heart.

'Why are you out here all alone?' she asked sleepily.

Mike smiled. He hadn't been alone. Not by a long shot. He met Lucy halfway as she walked barefoot towards him, yawning sleepily and rubbing her big blue eyes with the balls of her little fists. He picked her up and she snuggled into his warmth. By the time he had carried her upstairs to bed she was sound asleep. He tucked her in and went to his study... to stand by the window.

The vision of the girl dancing on the dunes was still with him. From his upstairs window he could clearly see the silvery outline of the rounded peaks which had been her stage. And through the young forest of trees barely half grown he could make out the small structure of Dune Cottage.

It was old and dilapidated but basically sound. He planned to move it to the back of the property to be used by his construction crews...

Mike's thoughts came to an abrupt end when a light suddenly appeared in Dune Cottage. Which, of course, was quite impossible. He'd had the electricity turned off and the place boarded up when he bought the estate. But even as he thought this, another light appeared. Someone was moving from room to room.

And there seemed to be only one logical conclusion as to who that someone could possibly be. The naked dune dancer!

CHAPTER TWO

THE beam from Mike's high-powered torch flooded
the smooth stretch of sand separating the mansion
and the cottage. He left the beach and climbed the
small embankment leading into the trees. He was a
big man but, despite his size, he moved with a silent
grace, a skill learned from a tribe of North American
Indians who had become his friends when he had been
searching for a suitable place to buy land for his ski
resort.

Dune Cottage was in total darkness now. Mike
cupped his huge hand around the beam of his torch,
leaving enough light to scan the area but not enough
to alert the intruder. He found what he was looking
for. The red MG was parked cosily under a tree. He
walked up to it and beamed it with his torch. The
tyres would soon need replacing. On the passenger's
side he noticed a child's straw hat and remembered
seeing a child with the erotic dancer. Mike straightened, switched off his torch and looked at the cottage.
Only the thought of the child kept him from entering
and demanding to know what had possessed the young
woman to break into his cottage.

A slender figure appeared suddenly at the window.
The glow from the moon touched her lovely features.
He could go up to her now, ask a few pertinent questions and demand that she be gone by first light in
the morning.

17

But there was such an air of vulnerability about the dancer, a curious mixture of a lonely kind of happiness as she gazed silently up at the moon, that Mike would have had to be made from stone to disturb her now. And he wasn't made from stone. Catherine moved slowly, reluctantly away from the window, her gaze lingering on the magical orb as though she was afraid it would somehow disappear if she didn't keep looking at it. Mike imagined her getting into bed, her eyes on the moon until sleep finally overtook her. He walked silently past the cottage and down to the beach. He would return first thing in the morning.

Catherine stirred restlessly in her bed. Ever since her dance on the dunes she had been filled with a delicious excitement. Never had she felt so free, so exhilarated, so totally in tune with nature. She had actually felt she could have touched the stars if only they had been a wee bit closer. The stars, the moon had been her *heavenly* companions but she hadn't felt *physically* alone. Her body had burned with a thrilling awareness, almost as if....

She slipped out of bed and went out to the veranda. Moonbeams danced on the incoming waves, its arc gradually widening until it hit the sand. Standing at the water's edge was a man. His back faced her as she stared disbelievingly down at him. He was tall and broad-shouldered, dressed more for the office than the beach in his white shirt and dark trousers. He must be a nearby resident, Catherine thought, taking a stroll to unwind after the pressures of the day. He held a torch in one hand and the other was thrust into his pocket. He seemed deep in thought and she sat down to watch him and to wonder what pressing problem occupied his mind.

Mike turned and started back along the beach in the direction of his home. A child's bucket caught his attention. It was in danger of being taken by the incoming tide and washed out to sea. As he bent to pick it up he saw it was loaded with seashells, and the bucket and the shells reminded him of Lucy. With the bucket in his hand he turned and headed up towards the cottage.

It was amazing how much better Dune Cottage looked in the moonlight. He supposed it looked better because the shutters had been removed. Was someone with her, someone other than the child? No, he sensed somehow that she was alone. And it would have been easy enough even for someone as slight as the dancer to remove the shutters. They had only been tacked on. Vandals weren't a problem here; not like the Sunshine and Gold Coasts. But security wasn't the main reason he had purchased this property for his resort. Hidden in a tropical forest up and beyond the cottage was a treasure. A cascade of rock pools, each spilling into the one beneath it and surrounded by towering ferns and a rich green moss, reached only by a succession of overgrown tracks, a perfect hideaway for his pampered guests.

As Mike got closer to the cottage it suddenly occurred to him that it was strange none of his staff had noticed that the cottage had been broken into. But maybe it wasn't so strange after all. The trees completely blocked it from view and only his bedroom and study faced in this direction. The dancer and the child could have been living here for quite some time undetected.

Catherine had seen the man pick up Jessie's bucket and appreciated him rescuing it from the waves. She had expected him to simply place it above the high-water mark where it would be safe. She certainly hadn't expected him to march straight up to the cottage with it dangling rather incongruously from his huge hand.

She pressed her back into the chair, her heart thumping wildly as he got closer. Should she stand up, meet him halfway, take the bucket from his hand and thank him for his thoughtfulness? Or should she simply sit here, hidden from his view by the veranda rail and the rustling palms? He would probably place the bucket on the bottom step and leave without ever knowing she was even there. Even if he put it on the top step, he still mightn't notice her, not if she didn't move, didn't breathe.

Her breath caught in her throat and she wasn't breathing. He climbed the first step, then the second. He was tall and ruggedly built, with a hard, uncompromising face, the look of a survivor, a hunter, one who licked the odds. His straight black hair fell over a wide, intelligent forehead, almost touching the arrogant arches of equally black brows. His nose was long and straight, the cheekbones high and wide, and despite his rugged masculinity he had a lean, hungry look, as though the prey he captured would never satisfy his appetite. His white shirt was in startling contrast to the deep tan of his skin which told her this man was born to the outdoors.

He was on the veranda floor now and bent to place the bucket by the door. Catherine's nostrils quivered with his intoxicating clean male scent. Her heart thumped so loudly she was certain he would hear it. But it was her small intake of breath which alerted him to her presence. He straightened and looked fully into the startled hazel of her eyes, and his own were equally jarred by the sheer force of that collision.

Both remained motionless, frozen in time as they stared at each other. His were the bluest eyes Catherine had ever seen. Long, spiky lashes made them appear almost black. She shivered but it wasn't from fear. Instinct told her this man was no rapist, no murderer. She was consumed with the eerie sense of precognition, almost as if she *knew* this man, had known him always.

Catherine continued to stare up at him, her eyes wide and wondering, her lips slightly parted as she took in the dark, sensuous looks, the gleaming white teeth behind lips which made her wonder... made her wonder what it would be like to be kissed by him, ravished by him...! She shook her head and felt her hair against her bare shoulders. If she had met this man before, she knew she would remember the exact time, the exact place, for he was totally unforgettable!

He reached for her hands and pulled her to her feet. The contact was electrifying. A tremor swept through her and Mike mistook this for fear. Well, she had reason to be afraid. Breaking and entering was a serious business and he didn't intend treating it lightly.

'Enjoying your holiday?' he asked casually.

'Yes, very much so.'

'Been here long?'

'We've only just arrived.' She smiled rather shyly and peeped down at her hands, so pale and fragile, in the huge tanned enclosure of his own. She could hardly believe she was standing here, holding hands with a stranger who didn't seem a stranger, while a host of butterflies did cartwheels in her stomach.

'Renting the place?' Mike continued in that same casual tone.

'Oh, no,' Catherine breathed. 'We're guests.'

Mike's black brows rose dramatically above the midnight blue of his eyes. He supposed *guests* was one way of putting it. Such nerve! 'And who invited you?'

'Mr Donahue,' she stated almost proudly.

Mike nearly choked. 'And when did this happen?'

'About a couple of weeks ago.' She eyed him curiously. Such a lot of questions but then she supposed nearby residents liked to know who would be spending the summer with them. 'Mr Donahue is the sweetest, kindest man I know,' she added almost as though she thought this might be some sort of reassurance.

Mike had never before heard himself so described and he knew for a fact there would be many who would heartily disagree with such a description.

'A couple of weeks ago, hmm?'

'Yes, just——'

Mike released her hands and gripped her shoulders. 'You *lie!*'

Catherine stared up at him, her face growing pale under the soft moonlight. 'No, I'm . . .'

'I'm Donahue!' he snarled. 'And two weeks ago I was in Borneo!'

Catherine's eyes widened. No wonder she had thought she knew him. In a way she did know him, had met him, through her mother's letters. She had fantasised about him, conjured up his image over and over again, but not even her fertile imagination had prepared her for the man in the flesh or for what effect he might have on her. She raised a trembling hand to her chest and felt her thumping heart.

'You're Mike?' she asked weakly.

Mike ignored the ridiculousness of that question and continued to glare down at her upturned face. It was all he could do to keep from shaking her. And then she had the audacity to smile, actually smile into the face of his fury. His fingers bit into the soft flesh of her shoulders.

'I wasn't referring to you,' she said softly, 'when I used the words sweet and... and kind. I was referring to your father. Albert invited us here.'

Mike's blue eyes widened in astonishment. 'You know my father?'

'Well, I've never actually met him, but...'

Mike's eyes narrowed with renewed suspicion. 'Never actually met him?' he broke in.

'No, not actually.'

His eyes narrowed further still. 'And what does "no, not actually"... actually mean?'

'It means I haven't met him but I do know him. Through... through his letters.'

'*Through his letters!*' The storm clouds which had been gathering in Mike's eyes exploded with a terrifying fury. 'My father suffered a stroke a few months ago. He can barely manage to hold a pen let alone *write letters!*'

'That's not what I meant,' Catherine quivered as he shook her, his eyes scorching her face. 'Albert only *signs* his letters. He... he dictates them and——'

'*Good God*, woman, is there no end to your lies?' Mike asked raspingly. 'When one story fails you simply invent another!' His eyes lashed her shocked face. 'What is your name?'

'Catherine Mitchell,' she answered shakily, and waited hopefully for some sort of recognition. But there was nothing to indicate in his smouldering eyes that her name meant anything. He hadn't been informed that she had been invited to holiday at the cottage. He obviously hadn't been told anything about her at all. A sickening despair washed over her as she realised what that meant. He assumed she had helped herself to the cottage, *his cottage*. And had lied about knowing his father.

'Well, Miss Mitchell . . .'

'It's . . . *Mrs* Mitchell,' Catherine broke in, her despair mounting by the second.

Mike stiffened. So there *was* someone else, someone other than the child, enjoying the comforts, such as they were, of his cottage. His dark head swung towards the door and a new rage engulfed him.

'There's only myself and my child,' Catherine stated quietly as though reading his thoughts. 'My husband died a . . . a few years ago.'

She hadn't expected any sympathy, nor did she receive any. If anything, his eyes seemed to grow even colder. 'Life can deal some pretty rough blows,' was all he said and Catherine nodded, well aware of the blows life had already dealt him.

'Yes, it can,' she quietly agreed.

'I imagine it's been a struggle raising a child on your own?'

Catherine hesitated. Had she misjudged him? She eyed him warily. 'It hasn't been easy,' she agreed.

'Finances would have been a problem,' he suggested.

'At times . . . most of the time . . . yes.'

'I saw your little girl today. She couldn't be more than seven or eight?'

Catherine's eyes widened. 'You were the man in the Jaguar?'

'I was.'

'I . . . I didn't recognise you. You were wearing dark glasses and . . .' She chewed on her bottom lip. Mike's eyes had seemed to grow even colder as he watched her. She thought back to what he had just asked her. 'Jessie's seven. She will be eight next week.'

'So there's still a long road ahead,' he stated matter-of-factly, his tone icy.

'Yes, but——' She was going to tell him about her new teaching position but he coldly cut her off.

'A road that could be made a great deal smoother . . . with the help of an elderly gentleman paving the way!'

Catherine gasped. The implication of his words rocked her. He smiled cruelly at her reaction and, before she could guess his intention, his hands snaked out and she felt herself being crushed against the steel strength of his body. He forced her lips apart, his mouth bruising, his tongue plunging into her soft moistness. His hands moved over her, moulding her against him, and she felt their scorching heat burning through her thin cotton nightie as he pressed her hips against his, grinding her against him.

She felt his strength, his power, his anger, the enforced contact stealing away her own strength, robbing her of her own will, and she clung to him, her fingers digging into the muscular shoulders, her thighs quivering against the rock hardness of his own. He pulled her nightie away from her shoulders and she gasped as his hands cupped her breasts, his thumbs moving over the tender erect nubs and she threw her head back, her hands moving into his thick, black wiry hair as he bent his head and took the throbbing peaks into his mouth, his sharp teeth rocking her body with the exquisite pain.

And then he thrust her away from him, his eyes still smouldering with an anger she couldn't understand, filled with a scorching contempt at her half-nakedness as Catherine struggled with her nightie, her cheeks burning with shame that she had done nothing to prevent this . . . this intimacy.

'I want you out of here by ten o'clock tomorrow morning,' he issued coldly and, with the command given, turned and left her.

Catherine stared after him, shocked and dazed by their brief encounter. He strode easily along the shifting sand as if it were the smoothest tiles. When he had disappeared from her view she turned and stumbled into the cottage. She lay on top of her bed and stared unblinkingly up at the ceiling. Not even the rhythmic lapping of the waves could soothe her shattered senses. It seemed impossible that only a short while ago she had been filled with such a delicious feeling of excitement, of happiness, of a sense of adventure. Now all she felt was a deep-rooted gloom.

Why hadn't Albert or her mother told Mike about herself and Jessie spending the summer at the cottage? Why was he back from Borneo? Had Albert taken a turn for the worse? That could explain why her mother hadn't been over and why Mike had cut his business dealings short. Her mind whirled endlessly with questions she couldn't possibly answer. After a sleepless night, Catherine had reached a decision. She and

Jessie would pay a visit to the mansion and find out what was going on. Obviously there had been a misunderstanding, a lack of communication. This sort of thing happened all the time, didn't it, to anyone?

Catherine held tightly on to Jessie's small hand as they followed the narrow path through the trees leading to the mansion. The closer they got to the imposing structure, the more nervous Catherine became. When they left the wood and stepped on to the green, manicured lawn, a tremor of apprehension whipped along her spine. A cobblestoned path led them directly up to the wide shaded veranda facing the ocean. The veranda jutted in and out, following the paths of the many rooms, and each room had a French window leading out to it. Clumps of patio furniture and huge earthenware pots filled with spectacular leafy green plants were scattered everywhere. It was like being in a hotel lobby or an indoor-outdoor house, so hugely grand was it. Magnificent white pillars stretched along the edge of the tiled veranda and, beyond that, golden sands rolled down to the crystal-blue water, capped with frothy white peaks. Despite the early hour, people were already setting up gaily coloured beach umbrellas while others were taking their morning strolls or paddling in the water. Sunbronzed surfers rode the waves further out to sea. Catherine's lovely hazel eyes rested on the spectacular sand dunes which hid Dune Cottage from the rest of the world. She took a deep breath, smoothed the skirt of her bright yellow sleeveless frock and, still holding Jessie's hand, stepped quietly towards the main door.

'Catherine! Jessie! Over here!'

Catherine and Jessie whirled at the sounds of their names being called out in a hushed whisper. Betty was frantically beckoning to them with one hand while cautioning them to be quiet with the other. In her mid-fifties, Betty still possessed a trim figure and a good rinse kept her short, stylish hair a natural-looking brown. She was dressed simply but smartly in a white summer frock with bright splashes of green. But despite her smart appearance Catherine detected signs of stress. She and Jessie hurried over to her, both of them receiving a quick hug.

'You shouldn't have come over here!' Betty blurted. 'Everything's gone terribly wrong.' She cast a quick, furtive look around and lowered her voice further still. 'Lucy, Michael's little girl, returned home a few days ago and you wouldn't believe the mischief she's been up to. And yesterday... yesterday Mike arrived! He sent a wire apparently but Mrs Beasley, for reasons known only to herself, chose not to inform either Albert or myself. And that dreadful woman has been holed up with Michael in his study since seven o'clock this morning telling him... telling him God only knows what!'

A sickening feeling spread quickly in Catherine's stomach. She had expected a simple misunderstanding but now she realised from her mother's distressed state that nothing simple was going on here.

'Mother, why wasn't Mike informed of Jessie's and my visit?' she asked quietly but refusing to whisper.

'There seemed no point. He wasn't expected home until after the holidays and you would have been gone by then. But I will tell him... just as soon as I get a chance. Mrs Beasley...'

'Mother, he already knows!'

Betty paled. 'What . . . what do you mean?'

'He came over last night. He . . .' She glanced quickly at Jessie, who was busy examining one of the potted ferns. 'He ordered us *out!*'

'What? Oh, no! This is terrible. Dreadful!' Betty wrung her hands in despair. 'But didn't you explain?'

Catherine sighed. 'I tried, but . . .'

A volley of piercing screams shattered the still morning air and brought their hushed conversation to a dramatic halt. Catherine and Betty stared in horrified alarm as Jessie doubled over in pain and collapsed in agony on to the veranda floor.

CHAPTER THREE

THE door burst open. Mike Donahue filled the frame, dressed in fawn-coloured silk shirt and chocolate-brown trousers. His smouldering blue eyes settled on Catherine sitting on the veranda floor with a hysterical Jessie cradled in her arms while Betty hovered over them, her face ashen.

'Help me,' Catherine begged, her eyes pleading with him. But he was already beside them, squatting on his haunches, his huge hands gentle as he pried Jessie's hands from where she was holding.

'I think she's been stung,' Catherine stated anxiously. 'She was standing over there by the fern. It might have been a...a wasp...or a hornet...I didn't see...'

'Definitely not the work of wasps or hornets,' Mike announced as he examined the small red welts on Jessie's arms and legs. He looked grimly around and his expression became grimmer still as he spied and picked up several hard and small pea-like pods from the tiled veranda floor. He straightened slowly, his cobalt-blue eyes gradually narrowing until they settled on a tall potted umbrella tree, with broad, glistening green leaves.

'Come here, Lucy,' he commanded in a low, firm voice.

A child emerged from behind the tree, defiance blazing from her big blue eyes. She was dressed in jeans and a T-shirt, her long blonde hair secured in a single plait draped over her shoulder. In one small hand was a drinking straw while the other was clenched into a tight fist by her side. Something escaped from her fist, dropped to the floor and rolled lazily around her feet. It was a small green pellet exactly like the ones her father held in his own hand. She walked slowly up to him, carefully avoiding his eyes but managing to glare at everyone else, especially Jessie. Jessie had stopped her sobbing and watched in morbid fascination as her tormentor made her slow approach. Catherine couldn't help feeling sorry for the child despite what she had done to Jessie.

Mike removed the straw and pellets from his daughter's hand, told her to apologise to Jessie and ordered her to her room where he would speak to her later regarding her behaviour. With haughty disdain, Lucy marched past him to the door where a handsome, well-dressed middle-aged woman with steel-grey hair and eyes to match gave her a sympathetic smile and a pat on the shoulder, almost as if she condoned Lucy's treatment of Jessie. It was the same woman who had managed to convey her hostility from the upstairs window, and, even before Mike addressed her, Catherine knew this formidable woman was his housekeeper, Mrs Beasley.

'Mrs Beasley, take the child to the kitchen and have Cook place ice-packs on those bumps.' He smiled down at Jessie. 'Cook is very nice. I wouldn't be at all surprised if she didn't find a big slice of chocolate cake for you!'

Mrs Beasley was obviously far from overjoyed at being appointed Jessie's guide into the kitchen and it was clear Jessie felt the same. She hung back, but when Mrs Beasley turned and disappeared into the house, Jessie reluctantly followed. The chance of a slice of her favourite cake was not something to be ignored. When the screened door had closed behind them, Mike turned to Betty.

'Why are you out here, Nurse?' he asked with a cold politeness which made Catherine bristle at his tone.

'The... the commotion...'

'The commotion is over. I suggest you retire to your duties.'

'Yes, sir.'

Yes, sir! Catherine couldn't believe it. Her mother was behaving like a humble servant instead of the highly trained professional that she was. She watched her mother quickly disappear through one of the many French windows and the sickening feeling in the pit of her stomach she had experienced earlier returned. Her mother had made her believe she was practically one of the family but it was becoming increasingly obvious that this simply wasn't so. Catherine had never been surrounded by so much hostility and she wondered how her mother could have endured it for so long. She turned to Mike, detesting his cold arrogance, forgetting that only moments earlier she had been warmed by his gentle kindness towards Jessie and impressed by his firm handling of his own daughter.

'Well!' she said stiffly. 'You've certainly managed to clear the deck. Everyone's gone.' She snapped her fingers. 'Disposed of...dispensed with...dispatched!'

'You're still here,' he curtly reminded her and glanced at his watch. 'But then, it's not quite ten o'clock!'

Being reminded of the hour of her eviction brought a wave of hot colour to Catherine's cheeks and forced her to remember why she was here. To sort out a simple misunderstanding, wasn't it, a slight lack in communication? *Hardly*! She felt as if she had stumbled straight into a hornet's nest ... or worse!

'Why didn't you tell me Nurse White is your mother?' Mike jarred her further by asking.

'I can't remember you giving me much of a chance to tell you anything!' Catherine returned swiftly.

'Well, you will have plenty of chances now,' he stated and placed a firm hand on the small of her back and led her towards the door. 'Mrs Beasley was showing me some very interesting accounts before you managed to disrupt my entire household!'

'Disrupt?' Catherine flared. 'Good heavens, we didn't get a chance to knock on the door before we were ... attacked!'

A deep flush rose on his cheekbones. 'My daughter and I have made our apologies,' he issued tightly and with his hand still placed firmly on her back escorted her down a long and very wide passage which seemed to continue endlessly.

'Where are you taking me?' Catherine panted as she struggled to keep up with his long-legged pace.

'To my study.'

His study! Where she would be *alone* with him? The overwhelming physical attraction she had felt for him last night had completely disappeared. She didn't want to be alone with him. The whole idea of it was totally disquieting.

'Why?'

'You'll see.' His hand left her back and gripped her wrist. She felt suddenly imprisoned. Panic rose in her

throat and she struggled to keep it down. They passed
handsomely furnished rooms, many of them obviously reserved for formal occasions, like the dining-
room which hosted an incredibly long table and a sea
of high-backed chairs. A young maid was polishing
the already gleaming table and looked up and smiled
when they passed.

Next to the dining-room was a lounge, with sump-
tuous furnishings, most of it expensive antiques and
softened by a carpet Catherine felt certain would cover
your feet. There were less formal rooms, rooms for
relaxing, with soft, plump sofas and chairs. It was all
so impressive...and so *quiet*! Where was the kitchen?
Catherine strained her ears for sounds of her daughter
but all she heard was the faint, barely discernible whirr
of a vacuum cleaner being operated somewhere in the
house. The sound was oddly reassuring but it didn't
help her to relax. Her grim-faced escort made certain
of that!

They arrived at a set of stairs. There had been
another staircase, in the grand foyer, majestic with
overhanging chandeliers and richly carved banisters
and railings, but this one was less formal, more intimate in its appeal. Again Catherine hung back.

'Come along,' Mike barked impatiently.

'I...I thought your study would be somewhere
down here,' she stammered nervously.

He frowned. 'What difference does it make?'

A lot of difference! Catherine silently railed. There
were *people* down here. Her mother, Albert and Jessie.
The cook, the maid...even Mrs Beasley. To be alone
with him was one thing. To be alone *upstairs* was quite
another.

'Jessie won't know where I am.'

'Peggy will tell her.'

'Peggy?'

'The maid in the dining-room.'

'Very well, then.' Any further protests would seem foolish and cowardly and she didn't want him thinking she was either. 'But there's no need to drag me to your study.' She looked pointedly at his hand encircling her small wrist. 'I can manage on my own, thank you very much!'

He released her and she walked beside him up the sweeping staircase. His shoulder brushed her arm and the effect was electrifying. Startled, she moved quickly away—too quickly—stumbled and would have fallen had he not grabbed and steadied her, his face a study in patience.

'Thank you,' Catherine mumbled, her face a fiery red. 'I...I'm usually not so clumsy.'

They climbed the rest of the way in silence, his hand once more gripping hers.

The landing at the top of the stairs branched off into separate corridors, leading to various wings of the grand mansion. Mike took one of them and Catherine found herself in a handsomely furnished hall, wide, with antique furnishings and huge framed pictures. The carpeting was thick and luxurious, their feet not making a sound against its plushness. They spoke not a word and Catherine's apprehension grew whenever she stole a glance at his grimly handsome face. At the end of the hall was a large cedar door and she knew even before they stopped at it that this was the door leading into Mike's study...the lion's den! He swung the door open and with a curt wave of his hand motioned for Catherine to enter.

Again she hesitated, her teeth clamped nervously to her bottom lip, but when she felt him stiffen with irritation she grabbed her courage and stepped past him and into the handsomely appointed room. The walls were panelled in a red cedar with impressive oil paintings decorating them. The armchairs and sofas were black leather and there were various tables holding brass lamps. A rich Oriental rug rested beneath a massive cedar desk, cluttered with a computer, fax machines, several files and an assortment of papers. On either side of the opened French windows which led on to the upstairs balcony, were floor-to-ceiling shelves lined with books. A soft, balmy sea breeze filtered in.

The door clicked shut behind her. Catherine whirled around, her heart pounding, her senses alerted to a hidden danger she instinctively knew she was facing. She could smell his intoxicating male scent and a faint whiff of his aftershave. His blue-black eyes were on her face but there was no warmth in their glittering depths. His eyes, his scent, the closed door were all disturbing enough, but there was something else, a feeling, which disturbed her far more.

He leaned against the door, his tall, lean solidity effectively barring any escape if that had been her intention. But it wasn't. She was anxious to clear up this business of the cottage, and the sooner the better. But she would have preferred doing so in less private, intimate quarters.

'Well, it took some doing but we're finally here,' he said, his voice a soft mocking drawl.

'So we are,' she agreed, boldly holding his dark gaze. 'But tell me, Mr Donahue, are we to be here long?'

'That depends on you,' he returned harshly. 'After all, you're the storyteller!' The hard gleam of challenge in his eyes told her to hold her tongue, that any provocation on her part would be welcomed so he could retaliate in some way! He pushed away from the door and strode briskly to his desk. Catherine's eyes followed him, troubled, no longer bold. He circled the massive desk and stood behind it, the huge black leather chair waiting to receive him. On the other side of the desk a smaller chair was pulled straight up to it and on the desk space separating them were an assortment of accounts, bills. Catherine had seen enough of these devils to recognise them immediately. Obviously Mike and Mrs Beasley had been abruptly disturbed from their perusal of them when Jessie had screamed. But what had these accounts to do with her? And why should she care if they were interesting? He indicated the chair and motioned for her to sit.

'Thank you,' she murmured and crossed over to it. She felt his eyes on her, watching her, the feeling so acute that she became ridiculously aware of her body and the sudden warmth which engulfed her. It seemed to take forever before she finally reached the chair, and when she sat down she actually felt she was floating. Avoiding the eyes which were responsible for her discomfort, Catherine smoothed the skirt of her dress and carefully crossed her legs, making certain her knees were well covered. Only then did she finally look up at him, to meet the scrutiny of those cold, blue, glittering eyes. He didn't waste time on preliminaries but got straight to the point.

'When I returned home last night, after my brief encounter with you, my father's light was on. We had

a little chat. I asked him about you.' He paused and
Catherine's heart stood still. 'He denied knowing
you!'

An icy chill settled over Catherine, helped along by
the frost in Mike's eyes. Her throat felt dry and when
she opened her mouth to speak it seemed to grow drier
still. 'Well, I did tell you we've never met,' she reminded him, her voice strained.

'Indeed you did.' He came from around his desk
and perched on the edge of it, dangerously close to
Catherine. He stretched out his long legs, the fabric
of his slacks tightening against his hard muscular
thighs and the bulge of his manhood. Catherine
quickly averted her eyes while a pink flush stained her
cheeks. Her palms were damp in her lap.

'I asked him about an invitation,' Mike continued
relentlessly, 'an invitation inviting a young woman and
her daughter to spend the summer holidays at Dune
Cottage. He denied sending such an invitation. In fact
he seemed quite puzzled that I should even be asking
him such questions.'

Catherine looked helplessly up at the cold un-
yielding mask of Mike's face. 'I...I c-can't understand it,' she whispered in despair. 'Mother gave me
his note at my graduation and...and I sent one back.'

Mike's eyes narrowed shrewdly on her face.
'Graduation?'

Catherine nodded. 'A couple of weeks ago...I
graduated from teacher's college.' Her soft hazel eyes
appealed to him. 'Do you think...it could be
possible...that your father might have forgotten?'

'My father suffered a stroke but he's not *senile*!'

'I . . . I wasn't suggesting . . .' She wrung her hands nervously in her lap. 'It's just that . . . it seems so . . . so strange and . . .'

Mike pushed himself away from the desk so abruptly that Catherine jumped. He gathered up the accounts into a neat and tidy pile and then flicked through them, stopping at one and studying it thoughtfully, before moving on to the others. The rattling of the pink, blue and white squares in his hands made a dreadful sound against the electrifying tension which sizzled around them. He formed the accounts into the shape of a fan and held them in front of Catherine's eyes.

'Do you recognise these signatures?'

She studied the bold, uneven sprawls and nodded. 'Your father's signature.'

'The same as on your note . . . your invitation?'

Again she nodded. He placed the accounts back on to his desk and went to stand by the opened French windows. The soft sea breeze tugged at his hair. Catherine's fingers trembled in her lap. She knew what that dark, wiry hair felt like. His back was facing her, his hands thrust deeply into the pockets of his trousers, and his broad, powerful shoulders were slightly hunched. 'I'll tell you what's strange,' he said softly, without turning around to look at her. 'All those accounts, signed by my father, are for work done at Dune Cottage!' He turned slowly and fixed her with his eyes. 'Where will you be teaching?'

The abrupt change of topic caught her off guard . . . that and the way he was looking at her, like he already knew the answer to his question. 'B-Bundaberg,' she stammered.

He nodded. 'An easy fifteen-minute drive back and forth to Dune Cottage!' His voice was taut, tightly controlled.

Two hot spots of colour rose high on Catherine's smooth cheeks. Now she knew what this was all about...why she had been brought up here...why she had been shown the accounts. She rose tremblingly to her feet. 'Are you suggesting that the cottage was fixed up for me? That your father was...was *tricked* into signing those accounts, *tricked* into inviting us here?'

He didn't even have the audacity to look ashamed. 'It did occur to me,' he coldly admitted. 'Somebody has gone to a great deal of trouble turning Dune Cottage into a comfortable residence.' He looked pointedly at the accounts. 'The other possibility of course is that your mother was hoping to retire there.'

'How dare you?' Catherine was trembling with shock, hurt and rage. 'You're despicable!'

He didn't seem troubled by that at all. 'Your mother has been widowed for a great number of years. She can't work forever and naturally she would be concerned about her future. She would have to be considering possibilities and...'

He broke off when a knock sounded at the door. An expression of annoyance crossed his face as he issued a curt command to enter. The door opened and Betty entered. Catherine stifled a groan. Her mother couldn't have picked a worse time to make an appearance. Betty closed the door behind her, offered an apologetic smile at having disturbed them and walked briskly over to stand by Catherine. There was no trace of her earlier humbleness. She addressed Mike.

'I hope you don't mind me barging in like this, but when I heard my daughter was up here I thought I should come up and apologise for not formally introducing you. With both of you arriving yesterday, practically on each other's heels ...'

Betty's speech came to a dramatic halt when she saw the accounts on Mike's desk, directly beneath her eyes. Catherine's breath caught in her throat and she couldn't breathe. To her utter amazement, Betty simply reached down, picked up the accounts and held on to them as though they belonged to her. Catherine stole a cautious glance at Mike. If he was surprised by her mother's action, he was certainly concealing it well.

'Albert and I have been looking everywhere for these,' Betty explained. She flicked casually through them, stopping at one the way Mike had and continuing on. 'We thought we had placed them in Albert's desk ... there's a query on some paint he had returned ... but when we looked, they had disappeared.' She added as a plausible excuse. 'Maybe Mrs Beasley found them and gave them to you, thinking they were household accounts?'

Well done, Mother! Catherine tossed a triumphant look at Mike. See! her expression said. There's been no conspiracy, no foul deed committed. Mike caught and correctly interpreted her look. His eyes hardened.

'Mrs Beasley gave them to me, but not because she thought they were household accounts. She was concerned about the expense going into the cottage for no apparent reason. Why wasn't I, or anyone else for that matter, informed of the work going on?'

'We didn't think anyone would be particularly interested,' Betty replied. 'Albert and I pretty much keep to ourselves. We don't bother much with the others. And . . . and we thought you would be pleased with the work done, a small thank-you on your father's part for having him here and employing me to take care of him.'

A dark hue spread across Mike's hard cheeks. 'My father knows me well. Well enough to know I don't require thank-yous.' His eyes narrowed on Betty's face. 'Tell me the real reason why Dune Cottage has received so much attention.'

Catherine's earlier jubilation was rapidly fading. She knew Mike had been weighing her mother's every word, every nuance, every gesture, searching for flaws no matter how slight. And now it appeared he had finally found one. She waited anxiously for her mother's reply.

'Well,' Betty began slowly, a pretty blush staining her cheeks. 'I . . . I guess we did it for ourselves, for Albert and me. You see, about a month ago, we went for a walk following the little path through the wood. We came out at the cottage. I had never seen it before and your father explained it was the original home-stead on your estate. It's such a dear little place and we sat on the veranda and . . . and talked about how we would fix it up if it was ours. We went there quite often, whenever Albert was feeling strong enough, and we sort of pretended it was ours, our own little place, and we decided to go ahead with our plans. We had tradesmen come when Mrs Beasley and the gardener had their days off.' She added smilingly. 'We enjoyed watching it take shape without anyone being the wiser.' And then, seriously. 'I apologise for not writing and asking your permission for my daughter and grand-daughter to holiday at the cottage . . .'

Mike waved her apology aside. 'Obviously you had my father's permission?' Betty nodded. 'Then that's good enough.'

Betty brightened obviously relieved. 'It means so much having them here, close by...'

Again he brushed her words aside. 'You could have had them stay here.' They discussed her like she wasn't in the room.

'Well, your father did suggest it but when we mentioned it to Mrs Beasley she said that you were expecting several guests over the Christmas period.'

'I'm sure there would still be room.' He turned to look at Catherine. 'But something tells me your daughter would prefer the privacy of the cottage.'

Betty smiled fondly at Catherine. 'Would you, dear?'

Catherine was feeling uncomfortable. Mike was being far too congenial. Avoiding his dark, all-seeing eyes, she returned her mother's smile. 'Yes, we're quite happy, thank you,' she answered stiffly, her 'thank you' including them both.

Betty was elated. 'So it's all right, then? They can stay?'

'They can stay.'

Catherine felt her mother relax at her side and wondered why *she* couldn't relax. The storm was over, wasn't it? The misunderstanding cleared. But it had seemed *too easy*! Mike was regarding Betty with a cold considering expression on his handsome face. Catherine tensed when he spoke.

'Does my father suffer serious lapses of memory?' he demanded to know.

'Not what I would describe as *serious*,' Betty replied, her tone truthful, professional. 'But his medi-

cation does affect him to some degree.' She added as
an afterthought. 'Especially his evening medication.
He can be pretty forgetful after that . . . even mildly
disorientated.'

'I see.' His eyes briefly met Catherine's and she saw
the pain he was feeling for his father reflected there.
'Thank you, Nurse.'

Betty knew she had been dismissed. Catherine suspected she had been as well and followed her mother
to the door.

'Catherine. One moment, please.'

Catherine turned to face him while Betty let herself
out the door, closing it quietly. Mike was sitting in
his huge, black, soft leather chair behind his desk,
his long tanned fingers forming a pyramid against his
broad chest. For several spine-tingling seconds his eyes
held hers and she felt the full potency of those all
compelling orbs.

'Enjoy your holiday,' he stated softly.

'Thank you.' Her smile was relieved. She didn't
expect an apology for having been misjudged. After
all, it had been as she had thought: a simple
misunderstanding.

His eyes hardened. 'Just don't get too comfortable!'
he added with a warning growl.

Catherine's smile vanished.

CHAPTER FOUR

DON'T get too comfortable, Mike had warned. Well, Catherine certainly had no intention of spending her entire holiday being uncomfortable! She planned to enjoy every minute of it, and part of that enjoyment included gardening. She and Jessie freed the hibiscus shrubs of their choking tangle of creeping ivy and long, tough grasses. A sturdy kitchen knife was used to cut out the dead wood and scissors found to prune the bushes into shape. Jessie carted the debris to the edge of the driveway, the beginnings of a compost pile. There was an empty window-box outside the kitchen window. Petunias would look great there and, using Jessie's bucket and shovel, earth was collected and the box filled. In fact petunias, pink and white ones, would look absolutely wonderful in the newly dug-out garden surrounding the cottage. They hopped into the MG and drove into the village.

Catherine saw him immediately. Mike was strolling leisurely along the paved walk, head and shoulders above the other passers-by. He looked fresh and immaculately handsome in a short-sleeved navy blue shirt and cream-coloured trousers. She knew how the deep blue of that shirt would enhance those incredibly blue eyes and a small sigh escaped her lips. Newspapers were tucked under his arm and he held on to Lucy's hand. Lucy was licking a triple-scooped chocolate ice-cream cone.

Catherine parked the car in front of a grocery shop with a display of seedlings arranged outside. She selected half a dozen punnets, three pink and three white. The shop assistant placed them in a flat box for her and, when they stepped on to the footpath again, they came face to face with Mike and Lucy.

For several seconds Catherine could only gaze helplessly up at him while her heart crashed against her ribs. He smiled down at her, his teeth a gleaming white against the tanned bronze of his skin. And then he reached out and collected a dried twig from the shining mane of her chestnut-coloured hair.

'Been rolling in the grass?' he drawled, and dropped the twig into the box. The half-opened little petunias blinked up at him. His eyes suddenly hardened. 'What are you planning to do with those?'

'Why, plant them...'

'It's not necessary.'

His harsh tone irritated her. 'Jessie and I like pretty things growing around us.' She reached for Jessie's hand. Jessie was making cross-eyed faces at Lucy who was taking long, exaggerated licks of her cone. 'Come along, Jess.'

'I hope that makes you sick, you little piggy,' Jessie growled at her as Catherine took her away.

Catherine's face was burning. She might be Mike's guest but she was an appreciative one. Why would he object to her planting a few petunias to brighten up the place? After all, the flowers weren't permanent. They would have finished flowering by the time she and Jessie left. She hurried along, knowing he was watching her, feeling his eyes boring into her back. It was a warm afternoon and even though she was dressed lightly in white shorts, sandals and a thin cotton T-shirt she felt uncomfortably hot.

'Where are we going now, Mummy?' Jessie wanted to know. And it was only after her child had spoken that Catherine realised they had left the MG parked in front of the grocery shop! Feeling foolish and knowing Mike was the cause of it, Catherine was reluctant to turn back. She didn't want him realising he had managed to unsettle her. In front of them was a sporting goods shop with bicycles for hire.

'I thought we would look at the bikes,' Catherine muttered and joined a small group of young people who were negotiating with a blond, sunbronzed, athletic-looking shopkeeper about his rates. The shopkeeper gave a long appreciative glance at Catherine and told her he would be with her shortly. In the meantime she was free to browse. Bicycles joined by bench-like seats, with brightly coloured overhead canopies and designed for two people to ride, took her attention. It would be fun for her and Jessie to try some day. The sunbronzed Aussie finished with his clients and hurried over to Catherine. She enquired about the rental rates, still very much aware of a set of dark blue eyes watching her. Even the fine hairs at her nape were being affected!

A shadow fell over them and even before Catherine looked up she knew they had been joined by Mike. He reached for her box and took it from her trembling hands. 'These won't be very pretty if you let them dry out in the hot sun,' he growled, and before she could utter a protest he had started walking down the footpath towards her car. Catherine offered the shopkeeper an apologetic smile and, clutching Jessie's hand, hurried after him.

'How dare you?' she spluttered when they had reached his side. 'So rude!'

He ignored her comment and, holding the small box with one hand, opened the door of the MG with the other. Jessie slid in and he placed the box on her lap. Jessie grinned up at him, then proceeded to examine the seedlings. Mike straightened and his eyes swept over Catherine. She returned his look with an indignant one of her own, her pulse racing.

'The next time you decide to stroll around the village streets,' he stated with a significant lift of his brows, 'you might consider wearing something a little less provocative!'

Catherine gasped and her cheeks flooded with colour. How dared he make such a comment about her attire? She dressed the way she felt: a tourist enjoying the sub-tropical climate. 'Are you suggesting that I wear trousers and a woolly jumper up to my neck!' Her voice trembled as she added, 'Is that what you meant by not getting *too comfortable*? You...you would have me die from *heatstroke*?'

'Don't be ridiculous!' he snarled. His eyes made a sweeping journey over the long, slender length of her legs, resting on the hem of her brief shorts, before moving up to the firm swell of her breasts, naked under her T-shirt. The erect peaks pushed invitingly against the thin fabric. His eyes smouldered with a sensuous flame but when he spoke his voice was decidedly cool. 'A dress would be more suitable... and some underwear!'

Stunned and humiliated, Catherine watched, eyes blazing as he strolled to the Jaguar parked further down the street. Furious with herself for allowing him to get the best of her, Catherine got into the MG and shot away from the curb at a speed not to be recommended. Jessie and Lucy poked their tongues out at each other as the MG roared past the Jag.

By the time the petunias had been planted in the window box and in the soil surrounding the hibiscus shrubs, buckets of water filled and poured around the seedlings, Catherine's temper had been restored to its usual good order. She had even managed to push Mike to the back of her mind, determined that nothing and no one would spoil their holiday. They swam in their own sheltered cove, collected shells, took their meals to eat on the veranda, throwing crusts to the seagulls, and in the evenings they read or played board games.

The petunias had opened their little heads more, and there were now beautiful splashes of pinks and whites to add to the coral of the hibiscus and the green of the rustling palms and the not-so-green lawn.

In fact, the lawn was causing Catherine a great deal of concern. It wasn't a real lawn, at least not in the accepted sense of the word. No doubt all the land had been pasture before being sold and the magnificent waterfront homes built. A great deal of money and time would be needed if she was ever to get it to the beautiful, lush green surrounding Mike's home. Well, she didn't have the money but she did have the time. All she really needed was a lawnmower and a hose. A good mowing and a soaking would be a start. Surely Mike's gardener would have a spare hose lying about, and maybe even a mower?

There was only one way of finding out. Throwing a shirt over her bikini and with Jessie in tow, Catherine followed the path through the wood. That odd nervousness she had experienced before when approaching the mansion returned, but she pushed it

firmly aside. After all, she wasn't going anywhere near
the sprawling splendour. The garden shed was located
well away from it. Besides, last time she had been on
a very important mission. This time she only wanted
to borrow a garden hose and a lawnmower.

A peaceful serenity surrounded the estate. Birds
chirped in the branches of the graceful old trees and
honey-bees droned sleepily among the flowering
shrubs. Catherine and Jessie followed a cobblestoned
path leading up to the garden shed, the path neatly
trimmed, the thick, green, luxurious grass growing up
to it.

The garden shed was covered with rich reddish
brown cedar shingles. It had several small windows
and, while the door was open, no one seemed to be
around. Catherine poked her head inside and called
out a greeting but there was no response. Jessie darted
off to chase a butterfly and Catherine warned her to
stay close by. She entered the shed and called out
again. On pegs above a meticulous work-bench were
several coils of garden hose. On the other side of the
large, dark interior were garden utensils including
mowers of various shapes and sizes. Sealed bags of
fertiliser stood in a corner and next to them were
wheelbarrows, big and small. Rakes, hoes and spades
were placed in a neat row, secured in a rack. It was
truly a gardener's mecca. Catherine turned to leave
the shed when she heard voices. Approaching was
Mike, dressed in a pale grey business suit, white shirt
and with a briefcase tucked snugly under his arm.
His companion was a middle-aged burly-looking
gentleman, wearing work overalls. Catherine assumed he was the gardener she had been looking for.
She stepped out of the shed and both men stared at

her in surprise, the gardener's expression openly curious, Mike's face tight-lipped and grim.

'What are *you* doing here?' Mike demanded to know.

Catherine flushed hotly at his tone. 'I came over to see if I could borrow a hose ... and a mower.'

Mike's eyes trailed over her and her skin tingled, making her wish she *were* wearing trousers and a woolly jumper instead of her bikini covered with a shirt. His eyes seemed to bore right through to her flesh and the effect was totally unnerving.

'There was a report from the house that someone was breaking into the shed,' he stated harshly.

'One would hardly need to break in,' Catherine returned boldly. 'The door was open.'

His eyes flashed. 'If you wanted to borrow something, why didn't you go to the house?'

'Because I didn't want to borrow anything from the house!'

Mike turned abruptly to the gardener. 'Fetch a hose for Mrs Mitchell, please, Grieves.' His voice was clipped.

Catherine stepped aside for Grieves to enter. He reappeared a few seconds later with a coil of hose.

'May I borrow a lawnmower, too, please?'

Grieves turned to look uncertainly at Mike.

'Grieves will mow the lawn at the cottage,' Mike curtly informed them and turned to leave.

'I want to mow it *myself*!'

He turned back to look at her, his eyes glittering angrily. She stared back at him, her own eyes blazing defiance. For several seconds they held each other's look, Grieves forgotten. 'I ... I would enjoy doing it

myself,' Catherine finally broke the tense spell. 'If you
don't mind,' she added almost in a whisper.

Mike nodded to Grieves and without a further word
strode across the manicured lawns and into his waiting
Jag. Only when he had driven away did Catherine
realise she had stopped breathing. Her breath was ex-
pelled in a long, lingering sigh.

Grieves loaded the mower and hose into the back
of his utility truck and offered Catherine a ride back
to the cottage. Catherine thanked him and called
Jessie, knowing her daughter would greatly enjoy
riding in the back of a truck. Grieves swung her up
and in and Catherine climbed into the cabin beside
the gardener.

'Can't say as I blame you for wanting to mow the
grass yourself,' Grieves remarked cheerfully as they
drove along. 'No sweeter perfume in the world than
the smell of freshly mown grass blowing up at you.'

He unloaded the mower, adjusted it for her, told
her it was light and easy to use but if she had any
problems she knew where to find him. As he climbed
back into the utility, Catherine thanked him and
casually asked him a question.

'Who reported that someone was breaking into the
garden shed?'

'Mrs Beasley, the boss's housekeeper.'

Catherine nodded. That was who she'd thought it
would be.

It didn't take long to mow the lawn and, when it
was finished, it looked remarkably improved. A good
drenching with the hose and it looked better still.
Catherine scooped out weeds and wished she had
thought to borrow some trowels but decided not to

go back. She didn't think it would be wise to push her luck.

After a few days and several long soakings the grass had turned a healthy green. The petunias were in full bloom and with the hose coiled around the garden tap and a blue tarpaulin retrieved from the boot of her car covering the lawn mower, Catherine felt quite settled in. The cottage became home to herself and Jessie. They had never felt happier.

'May we climb over the dunes and walk on the other side of the beach?' Jessie wanted to know late one afternoon when they had been there for almost one full week. It had been an especially hot day and they had spent most of their time sheltering under the shade of the palms. Now, with the sub-tropical sun high in the sky, it had become a bit cooler. Catherine yawned sleepily and stretched. A walk would do them good.

'All right,' she agreed, and tied a lime-green sarong around her waist, covering her yellow bikini bottoms but leaving the top to serve as a halter. She got Jessie a T-shirt to put over her little bikini and, with sun-glasses to shade their eyes and straw hats to protect their heads, climbed the steep dunes, stood on the top and looked over the other side.

The beach was swarming with people, a sure sign that the long holiday season had truly begun. They had seen the odd person on their own little beach but not many ventured to climb the dunes. Holding hands, they slipped and slid down to the smooth stretch of beach. Catherine silently vowed she wouldn't look at the mansion when they passed it. She would walk straight by, as if she had ever forgotten it existed. But when they drew closer her eyes were drawn to the stately structure as though pulled by a magnet. No

one was sitting on the wide, shaded veranda and there
were no faces at the windows. She knew Mike had
flown to Sydney the day he had confronted her at the
garden shed. While she never asked for information
about him, her heart always managed to do silly things
like hopping up and down whenever Betty volun-
teered any titbits on her occasional visits to the cottage.
And through Betty she had learned he was back. A
strange feeling swept over her as they passed his home.
She refused to admit the feeling was disappointment.
Disappointment that she hadn't seen him.

Their stroll took them to the opposite end of the
beach where a volcanic rock enclosure formed a pool.
A short ramp led to a park equipped with barbecues,
slides and swings. The park, like the beach, was
crowded, but Jessie managed to have fun on the
swings. On the way back, they walked in the water,
the incoming waves frothing around their ankles.

The tides were becoming bigger, more forceful,
known locally as the Christmas tides. Even as they
walked, the surf grew stronger, the froth turning to
splashes, hitting at their legs and wetting Catherine's
sarong. Several times they narrowly missed being
knocked down by body-surfers as the rolling waves
swept them into shore.

'Be careful, Jessie!' Catherine cried out a warning
as Jessie raced ahead of her, dancing over the waves
in a childish glee.

It was then that she saw him. He had just stepped
down from his steps leading on to the beach. He
strolled like a tall, proud, magnificent warrior towards
the pounding surf. His powerful, tanned body was
clad only in a pair of scarlet board shorts, a towel
strung casually across one broad shoulder. As he ap-

proached the water's edge, he dropped the towel and
stared out to sea, his black hair tossed by the wind.
Catherine stood quite still, her heart racing, her mouth
dry as she watched him, oblivious to everything else
except the man who held her spellbound. With one
smooth, graceful motion, he dived cleanly under a
huge wave and emerged metres from the shore. He
looked over his shoulder checking the waves, allowing several small ones to pass by before she could
actually feel his body tense as a monster loomed and
crested far out to sea. His timing was perfect. He
caught the monster, wrestled it, and rode it into shore
in a superb execution of the finely tuned body-surfer.
Catherine let out her breath in a soft, trembling sigh
as he picked himself up, muscles rippling, and dived
again into the pounding sea. She tore her eyes away
just long enough to check on Jessie but her child was
nowhere to be seen.

'Jessie?' she called, and hurried along the shore,
her eyes frantically searching. There were so many
children. Most of them seemed to be Jessie's exact
size, with Jessie's colour of T-shirt.

'*Jessie!*' Her voice rose in panic as her search swung
from the beach to the surf. The waves were enormous,
threatening, crashing on to the shore with a deafening
roar. A straw hat floated on a wave and Catherine's
eyes rounded with fear. *Jessie's hat!*

Catherine tore into the surf. The waves rushed at
her, knocked her down, refused to allow her to get
up. Salt water stung her eyes, filled her mouth.
Suddenly Mike was there, his hands on her arms, and
she felt herself being pulled free of the powerful waves.
He picked her up and carried her to shore and plonked
her rather ungraciously onto her feet.

'If you can't swim, stay clear of the water,' he ground out and turned to re-enter the pounding surf.

'No, *wait*!' Catherine screamed after him. She grabbed his hand. 'It's *Jessie*! I... I've *lost* her!' Her eyes were rounded with fear and her voice was filled with panic. 'She must have gone into the water. Or... or maybe a wave dragged her out.'

'Jessie is safe. She's right behind you, watching some children build sand castles.'

Catherine stared at him. 'S-safe?' She whirled to see Mike spoke the truth. Jessie was indeed watching a small group of children building in the sand. She turned back to Mike, relief making her feel quite weak. 'I... I lost track of her. There are so many people and... and when I didn't see her...'

A guilty flush stained her cheeks when she remembered why she had lost track of Jessie in the first place! Suddenly she didn't know where to look. Certainly not into those deep blue eyes, and definitely not at that tanned, broad chest with the silky black hairs clinging wetly to his skin. Nor at the strong brown columns of his legs planted firmly in the sand.

'It's easy to lose track of children on the beach,' he agreed and bent down to pick up the hat she had lost to the surf. 'Especially when something else takes your interest!' He handed her the hat and their fingers brushed briefly as she accepted it. Catherine quickly snatched her hand away, fingers trembling. Had he seen her watching him? she couldn't help but wonder. The wicked gleam in his eyes told her he had! Holding her head high, Catherine retrieved Jessie and hurried her along the crowded beach to the dunes. Mike watched them climb, a bemused expression darkening his eyes.

CHAPTER FIVE

JESSIE sat at the kitchen table and stared gloomily down at her birthday party list.

'My birthday's not going to be any fun tomorrow,' she grumbled. 'There's only going to be me, you, Grandma and Albert.' She sighed heavily. 'I'll be the only kid.'

'Why don't you invite Lucy?' Catherine suggested, knowing this was what Jessie wanted but wasn't willing to admit.

'What if she shoots me again?'

'I'm sure that was a one-off.'

'Well, what if she makes faces and calls me names?'

'I think you've done a bit of that yourself,' Catherine reminded her reproachfully.

'Well, what if I invite her and she says *no*?'

The ultimate insult. Catherine hid a smile. 'What if you invite her and she says *yes*?'

'So you think I should?'

'It's up to you.'

Jessie thought long and hard for a full three minutes and came to a decision. 'I'm going to invite Lucy,' she announced and got out paper and coloured pencils to design an invitation. When it was completed to her satisfaction, because it was important, after all, to impress Lucy with her artistic skills, Jessie set off to deliver it. Catherine silently prayed that Lucy wouldn't let her down. Three minutes later, Jessie returned.

'Come with me, Mummy, please,' she begged.

57

Catherine chuckled and laid down her gardening magazine. 'Think you might need a little back-up, huh? All right, poppet, just give me a minute and I'll be right with you.'

Her beige, loose fitting shorts, fresh white sleeveless blouse and brown leather sandals were suitable attire, she decided, and so with a quick brush of her shining hair and a dab of lip gloss Catherine was ready to help Jessie deliver the invitation. The compost pile was certainly growing to a respectable size, she noted with satisfaction as they passed it on their way to the path stretching between the young forest of trees. The grass clippings had helped, not to mention all the weeds and leaves. Grieves was using a 'ride-on' mower to cut the grass of the park-like lawns and waved to them as they stepped out of the wood and on to the cobblestoned path. Catherine and Jessie returned the greeting and the friendliness of the gardener cheered them. It was their third visit to the estate but the first time they had felt welcomed.

The feeling didn't last. Mrs Beasley answered their knock. Her reception was decidedly cool.

'Yes?'

'Good afternoon, Mrs Beasley,' Catherine greeted her politely. 'May we see Lucy for a moment, please?'

'Lucy is busy. I'm afraid she can't come to the door.'

'Oh, dear, what a shame,' Catherine demurred, then brightened. 'Perhaps we can go to Lucy.' She added quickly, knowing Mrs Beasley was about to voice another objection, 'Jessie has an invitation for her.'

'It's my birthday tomorrow,' Jessie announced importantly, and held up the pretty invitation.

Mrs Beasley reached for it. 'I'll see that Lucy gets it.'

Jessie whipped the invitation behind her back. 'I want to give it to her myself!' she announced stubbornly.

'Oh, very well.' She stepped aside and allowed them to enter. The young maid Catherine had seen dusting the dining-room table appeared in the grand foyer with an armful of towels. She smiled at them as she headed for the staircase. 'Peggy,' Mrs Beasley addressed her. 'Take Mrs Mitchell and her young daughter out to the pool, please. I believe Lucy is there with her grandfather and . . .' She glanced coldly at Catherine. 'And his nurse.'

'Certainly, Mrs Beasley.' Peggy placed the folded towels on a handsomely carved, high-backed chair and with another friendly smile told them to follow.

'Don't mind Mrs Beasley,' Peggy told them as they made their way through a labyrinth of passages on their way to the pool. 'She might seem a grouch but she's got a heart of gold.'

'Really?' Catherine was surprised.

'She's very protective of the family,' Peggy continued to confide. 'There's nothing she wouldn't do for them.'

Had the words been spoken by anyone other than this obviously friendly and cheerful young woman, Catherine would have considered them some form of threat, or warning. Nevertheless, a chill still managed to whip down her spine.

They entered a cool, tiled area, designed for outdoor entertaining even though it was covered with a roof and the walls screened. There was a huge bricked-in barbecue and spit for roasting great portions of meat. An impressive bar was built into one side of the room and behind it a caterer's kitchen, fully equipped. There

were groupings of tables and chairs and, when these
were pushed back, the floor would be big enough for
dancing. Across the gleaming black and white tiles,
the pool area began, protected for privacy with leafy
potted palms and umbrella trees. Peggy led them
through this indoor-outdoor tropical jungle to a magnificent pool which meandered through ferny glades,
tiny islands, rock slides and fountains. Chaises-
longues, protected by overhead striped umbrellas, were
strung around this magnificent engineering feat, which
Catherine later learned was designed and built by
Mike. There were also groupings of tables and chairs,
these too shaded by umbrellas. In a protected corner
of the enclosure sat Catherine's mother, reading from
a book of poetry to an elderly white-haired gentleman
who appeared to be dozing in his comfortable lounge,
and perched on the pool's edge was Lucy, looking
restless and bored. Betty and Lucy looked up in
startled surprise when Peggy led Catherine and Jessie
over to them.

Albert hadn't been dozing at all. His bright blue
eyes made a swift appraisal of Betty's daughter and
granddaughter and Catherine knew, when he smiled
at them, that they too had met with his approval.
Despite his obvious frailty, his grip was surprisingly
strong when he shook Catherine's hand. She knew
the snow-white hair would have once been as black
as his son's was now, and the eyes were still as blue.
Albert was a handsome gentleman, dignified and
strong. Catherine could exactly see why her mother
had become so attached to him.

Lucy was suspiciously eyeing what Jessie held in
her hand and Jessie was deliberately teasing her by
not showing her *exactly* what it was.

'Don't you have something for Lucy, Jess?' Catherine prompted, hiding her exasperation. Jessie handed the invitation over. Lucy read it, folded it and placed it on a table beside them which held a huge jug of lemonade and a platter of snacks.

'Well?' Jessie growled. 'Do you want to come or not?'

Lucy shrugged her little shoulders. 'Maybe I do...or maybe I don't.'

Jessie valiantly hid her disappointment. This wasn't working out the way she had hoped. 'Well, I don't care one way or the other,' she sniffed. The three adults exchanged amused glances. The situation was saved by the sound of firm footsteps walking across the tiles.

'That will be Mike!' Albert exclaimed as he recognised the sound of his son's step, his eyes warmed by the prospect of a visit. Mike stepped out onto the pool enclosure and immediately found Catherine's eyes. A warm flush radiated through her and she was powerless to turn away. Even surrounded by their parents and children, a mere look could cause her body to react in a way that was almost shameful, and as his eyes held hers she could actually feel the warmth of his touch, his body pressed against hers, the memory of a bruising kiss! Mercifully, he turned away and greeted the others. Catherine leaned back in her chair, the tension draining out of her. He walked over to them, and she feasted her eyes on the true magnificence of this powerful man. He was dressed casually in white trousers and a short-sleeved olive-green shirt, unbuttoned at the strong brown column of his neck. She half listened as he spoke to the group, the words meaning nothing, the sound of his voice everything. Her eyes fastened on to his hands as he picked up the jug and poured himself a glass of lemonade. Those hands . . . and how they had made her feel! And suddenly it occurred to her that he hadn't been surprised she and Jessie were out here, sitting down, enjoying the hospitality of his family and patio. And then she realised that of course he would already have known. Mrs Beasley would have informed him.

'Take a look at *this*, Daddy!' Lucy said, and handed him Jessie's invitation. Catherine held her breath as he read it. He would have been forewarned about the invitation, too, and she had no doubt that Mrs Beasley would have advised him against allowing Lucy to accept. He looked up from the childish print and straight into Catherine's anxious eyes. His eyes conveyed a silent message of thanks!

He turned to Jessie and placed his huge hand on top of her soft little curls. 'So your birthday is tomorrow,' he said kindly with a smile to match. 'And you will be eight years old.'

Jessie nodded and beamed up at him, her brown eyes openly adoring. He turned to Lucy. Her eyes were bright with jealousy.

'You have my permission to go, princess. Sounds like a lot of fun.'

'You can come too!' Jessie dismayed Catherine by saying.

'Jessie!' Catherine gasped, her cheeks turning scarlet. 'Lucy's daddy is a very busy man. Far too busy to come to your birthday.'

'As a matter of fact, I'm not.' There was a bold challenge in his eyes as he scored a hit with Catherine's. 'Tomorrow at two suits me just fine!' He picked up his glass and finished the last of his lemonade, thanked Jessie for her kind invitation and made his departure. Catherine stared after him. So he *had* been informed of their visit and Jessie's invitation. He had manipulated Jessie into extending her invitation to include himself. And Jessie had willingly obliged. After they had made their own departure and were in the privacy of the wood, Catherine gathered her daughter to her and gave her an exuberant hug!

'*They're here*!' Jessie excitedly announced. It was precisely two o'clock but Jessie had been waiting at the kitchen door for almost half an hour. She was dressed in her pale blue party frock, white shoes and socks, and Catherine had managed to tame her hair with the help of two pretty blue bows. Jessie looked adorable.

Behind her the table was stacked with plates of little sandwiches, cookies and cupcakes. A chocolate cake, decorated with candles, held pride of place in the centre of the table. Balloons and streamers hung from the overhead lamp. Catherine rushed out of her bedroom, wearing a white sundress with a wide yellow sash tied around her trim waist. Her hair bobbed around her bare shoulders and there was a vibrant glow in her eyes.

Jessie had already run outside and Catherine followed at a more sedate pace. Mike had opened the back doors of an impressive-looking beige Mercedes and Betty and Lucy were alighting. Mike helped his father from the front seat, steadied him and handed him his cane. Greetings were exchanged, especially to the birthday girl, and Betty loaded Jessie's arms with beautifully wrapped gifts from her and Albert. Mike

retrieved more gifts from the boot of the Mercedes
and handed them to Lucy to hold. She immediately
dropped them. Mike spoke quietly to her and she reluctantly picked them up.

Oh, dear! thought Catherine and hurried up to
them, relieving Lucy of the presents and telling her
how pretty she looked in her smart blue plaid dress
and the matching band holding back her long blond
hair. Lucy ignored the compliment and followed her
grandfather into the cottage. But within minutes there
were squeals of laughter and Catherine relaxed. She
had a feeling the party was going to be special, very
special.

Mike grabbed his navy blue jacket from the front
seat and swung it over his broad shoulder. His fresh,
crisp white shirt, maroon tie and grey trousers looked
superb. He smiled down at her upturned face and removed the presents from her arms. Her heart bounded
across her chest.

'Thank you for inviting Lucy to Jessie's party,' he
said. 'Lucy needs a friend.'

'It was Jessie's idea. I think they'll get along...once
they stop competing with each other.' A thought occurred to her. 'Would Lucy have come without you?'

'I don't think so. She's been behaving
rather...awkwardly at the moment. She might have
refused just to spite Jessie even though I knew she
wanted to go.'

So he *had* deliberately wrangled an invitation,
Catherine thought, to keep two little girls happy. Jessie
and Lucy ran out to collect the rest of Jessie's gifts
and raced back in with them. 'Grandma gave me some
clothes and Albert gave me a porcelain doll,' Jessie
yelled over her shoulder. 'Lucy and her daddy have

given me books and games. We're going to open them and play with them.'

'Kids!' Catherine muttered and grinned up at Mike. 'Don't you just love them?'

He chuckled, a warm, vibrant sound which did crazy things to her nervous system. 'Sometimes,' he agreed, and glanced around at the garden, the neatly trimmed lawn and the flowers in the window-box. 'You've certainly been busy!'

'I've enjoyed it.'

'Well, don't put too much effort into it.'

'It's not too much effort. I want to leave the place even nicer than it was when we arrived.' She added teasingly. 'Maybe then you will allow us to come back next holidays.'

'The cottage won't be here. I'll be moving it to the back of the property next to the road.'

'Moving it! But why?'

'Because I plan to build a resort here. Trucks and bulldozers will be working where we now stand.'

'A resort!' Catherine's face had turned pale.

He nodded. 'I'll use Dune Cottage as an office and eating mess for my construction crews.'

'Construction crews!' Catherine repeated hoarsely, and immediately pictured burly men with hard-toed muddy boots scratching the lovely pine floors and ruining the freshly painted walls with work schedules and posters of naked women. 'How ghastly!'

'Ghastly?' He shook his dark head and smiled down at her look of horror. 'The project will be exciting, but don't worry, your holiday is safe. I have another project on the boil at the moment...in British Columbia. I won't be starting the preliminary groundwork here until that one is well under way.'

Her eyes drifted to the veranda. Through the swaying palm trees she could barely see the girls playing with Jessie's new toys by Albert's and her mother's feet. 'Your father and my mother will have nowhere to go,' she said sadly. 'No little place to call their own.'

Mike touched her hair. 'What a little romantic you are, Catherine. They've got acres of gardens to wander through and . . .'

'But it's not the same. It all belongs to you. This does too but they . . . they've adopted it, made it theirs.' Her dark eyes were troubled as she gazed up at him.

His hand moved from her hair to cup the side of her cheek and his eyes lingered on hers. 'It won't be happening right away,' he reminded her, his voice husky. 'They will still have plenty of time to enjoy it.'

Catherine lost herself in the eyes which held her captive, eyes which were as blue and as powerful as the sky above and the ocean beyond. His eyes dropped from her face to the creamy stem of her neck, to linger on a tiny pulse beating frantically in the shadowed hollow of her throat. He lowered his head and she felt his lips there, and the wild, tingling sensation in the pit of her stomach raced up to her heart. She trembled at the strength of his body against the yielding softness of her own, his hard, muscular thighs pressed against the trembling weakness of hers. His eyes moved slowly upwards, to capture hers again, and her breath caught in her throat at the smouldering flames of desire burning in those deep blue orbs. His hands on her arms tightened in a passionate challenge and her heart skipped several beats as he drew her closer still.

'You're so beautiful, Catherine,' he husked against the softness of her cheek. 'So incredibly beautiful!' His mouth moved slowly to her lips and she felt the gentle pressure which was electrifyingly intoxicating, and her whole being flooded with desire.

His hands moved around to her back and she melted against him, the heat of his hard body surging down and through the length of her own. His mouth parted her lips and she welcomed his tongue and her whole world seemed filled with him. Her arms moved up and she entwined his neck, her fingers touching his skin and thrilling to the feel of wiry hair against the smoothness of his collar. He pressed her against him, his hands moving over her hips, clutching her buttocks, and they began to sway in a rhythm of ecstasy, their bodies in exquisite harmony.

'Mummy!' Jessie's voice rang out and penetrated Catherine's passion-fogged brain. 'Are we going to eat soon?'

Catherine pulled away with a guilty start. Jessie raced from the veranda steps and ran up to her. Catherine straightened her hair and her dress with trembling hands, avoiding Mike's eyes but knowing he was watching her. How could she have fallen so easily into his arms, forgetting, actually *forgetting* that there was a party, her child's birthday, waiting to happen?

'Everything's ready,' she told Jessie, her voice breathless, her breathing shallow, grateful that the child hadn't seen anything, had merely assumed Mummy had been chatting with Lucy's daddy. Jessie turned and raced back to the veranda.

'Everything's ready!' she shouted.

Catherine hurried to the kitchen door. Mike's voice
stopped her. She turned slowly. His black hair was
mussed and his tanned cheeks flushed. His teeth
gleamed white in his face. 'Need any help?' he asked
in a drawl, his voice still slightly thickened with
passion. Catherine shook her head, when all she
wanted to do was run straight back and into his arms.
She turned and fled into the kitchen as if the devil
himself were chasing her. He didn't follow her. He
picked up his jacket, brushed it off, swung it over his
shoulder and joined the little group on the veranda.

Catherine could hear them talk. Mike's deep-
timbred voice blending with his father's older, frailer
inflections; Betty's gentle tones and the squeals and
laughter from the two girls as they continued their
play with Jessie's newly acquired gifts. It all sounded
so pleasant, so warm, so... *family*! A soft smile
touched her lips and stayed there as she poured juice
into glasses, plugged the kettle in to make tea and
added sprigs of parsley to the platters of freshly cut
sandwiches.

The girls came in and she gave them each a plate
of sandwiches to carry out to the veranda. Catherine
followed with a tray filled with the glasses of juice,
tea cups and the pot of tea. She was almost at the
veranda when she heard Mike say he would be leaving
for Sydney on the early evening flight from Bundaberg
and would be away for at least ten days.

The words came as a shock. He had been away
before but she hadn't known until Betty had told her
and then she had treated it as *news*! News of his
whereabouts, and it had excited her to hear anything
about him at all. But this time she knew in advance;
knew he would actually be *gone*, and the very idea of

it filled her with a dreadful sense of loneliness. Her hands trembled and the teacups rattled. All eyes turned to look at her as she stepped on to the veranda.

But she was aware of only one set of deep blue probing orbs and she did everything in her power to avoid them. Mike rose from his chair and removed the tray from her shaking hands, watching her intently as she moved quickly away from the warmth of his body to stand by the veranda rail. The sea breeze lifted her glorious mane of shining chestnut hair from her cheeks, leaving only a few silky strands to cling against her flawless skin. Unaware of the captivating picture she made, she let her eyes move up to meet with his, the depth of her yearning shadowed by the sweep of her lashes, lending her an aura of mystery. His own eyes glinted with a mysterious light of their own and touched something deep within her, something which had never been touched before. The very air surrounding them became charged with the intensity which gripped them.

'Shall I pour, dear?'

The sound of her mother's voice effectively broke the heart-rending spell. Catherine took a deep breath like she had just returned from a great journey.

'Yes, please.' The cups of tea and the glasses of juice were handed around and the tasty sandwiches had soon disappeared. The conversation was light and congenial, Mike telling them a few adventurous stories about his time spent in Borneo, and as Catherine watched his easy rapport with his father she couldn't help wondering if there was a time when he would have discussed every single detail of his construction and engineering works with Albert, and knew he would have.

'Are we going to have my cake now, Mummy?' Jessie wanted to know, her eyes glowing with anticipation.

'Yes, darling, but not out here.' Catherine turned to the others. 'It's getting a bit windy so I think we should have the cake inside.'

They moved into the kitchen and took their places at the table. Mike remained standing, helping Catherine at the counter, a box of matches in his hand waiting to light the candles. The waves rolled and crashed on to the beach, matching the restless tempo of her pulsating heart. The candles were lit and Mike picked up the cake and handed it to her. Over the soft glow of the tiny flames their eyes met once more and the last of her defences melted away.

'Start singing,' Catherine smiled as she turned and carried the beautiful cake to the table. As she placed it in front of Jessie, Jessie looked up at her and her eyes were filled with love and gratitude.

'Thank you, Mummy,' she said softly, and impulsively grabbed Catherine's hand and kissed it. Tears of happiness sprang to Catherine's eyes and she quickly brushed them away as she returned her daughter's kiss. 'Happy birthday, darling.' And she sang the rest of the birthday song with a lump in her throat while Mike moved over to stand by her side.

'Close your eyes and make a wish!' Lucy commanded, and while Jessie had her eyes squeezed shut and her small brow was puckered in concentration, and before anyone could guess her intentions, Lucy quickly leaned forward and blew out Jessie's candles!

'*Lucy!*' Mike's sharp and angry voice broke the stunned silence. Jessie's eyes flew open. She stared in disbelieving horror at the tiny puffs of smoke spiralling

above her cake. She turned on Lucy, a small bundle
of fury.

'You're a mean, horrid little girl!' she shrieked, and
ran crying into her room. They could hear her muffled
sobs and the sounds tore at Catherine's heart.

'Gawd!' Lucy muttered. 'What a little baby. They
were only *candles*.'

And with that remark, Mike picked up his daughter,
slung her over his shoulder and marched out of the
cottage. Betty and Albert followed, Betty's face tight-
lipped and grim; Albert's filled with a sorrowful
shame. The door closed behind them. Catherine stared
at the burnt-out candles and went in to console her
daughter. The party was over.

CHAPTER SIX

CATHERINE stood at the edge of the dunes. Stars flickered above her from the midnight blackness of the sky. But she wasn't looking at them. Her soft hazel eyes were following another light, a flickering red light, weaving its way across the heavens.

Was Mike up there ... in that plane? she wondered, and, as she looked, her overwhelming feeling of loneliness intensified because she hadn't had a chance to say goodbye ... to wish him a safe trip and to tell him ... to tell him she would be thinking about him ... and waiting for his return.

She was still wearing the white sundress she had worn for the party but the yellow sash was now holding her hair back, tied into a bow at the nape of her neck to keep her hair from her face. A strong breeze had crept up and she welcomed it. It fanned her fevered body, the aching heat which burned within her.

The flickering red light disappeared but still she watched, thinking perhaps it might have drifted behind a cloud and would re-emerge at any second. And if it did, she would see it and it would be as if he were still with her. But the light was gone and finally she lowered her eyes, and the breeze muffled her heart-rending little sigh and swept it out to the sea to mingle with the restless moanings of the incoming tide.

Catherine turned and looked down at the cottage. It was in almost total darkness, the only light coming from the small lamp in the corner of the lounge. Jessie was asleep. They had put fresh candles onto her cake, a wish had been made, the candles blown out, a slice served to each ... and Jessie had carefully nursed her misery as only a child could and Catherine had been grateful when bedtime had finally rolled around.

Her eyes drifted to the corner of the lawn where Mike had kissed her, where she had kissed him, where together they had slipped out of this world and found a better one. One filled with nerve-tingling sensations, sensations she could still feel, deep within her, achingly sweet, erotic, a hot, throbbing dampness between her thighs which refused to go away, a pulsing tingling in her nipples which kept them erect and made her breasts ache and want to be held, to be drawn into a hot mouth, to feel his rough tongue and sharp teeth torturing them, the way he had that first night, when her body had been jolted into total awareness, total...

A car was making its way slowly down the drive. She knew it would be her mother. She had been expecting her the whole evening, knowing she would be concerned about Jessie and coming to check to see if her little granddaughter had survived her disappointment over the cake. Catherine wished she hadn't. Not now. Not when her whole body was charged with electricity, every raw nerve-ending sizzling with heat. She raised trembling hands to her fevered cheeks and took a deep, steadying breath. It didn't work. And the cooling sea breezes only seemed to fan the fires which raged within her. The car came to a halt. Catherine heard the muffled sound of a door being quietly shut. She wanted to run, to hide, and for several seconds her eyes darted wildly across the vacant dunes but there was nowhere, nowhere where she wouldn't be seen, where she could shelter herself, to protect what was happening to her until she could at least understand it herself.

Slowly, reluctantly, Catherine started towards the opposite edge of the dunes to make her way down to the cottage. A tall, dark figure was strolling across the moon-splashed lawn. Not towards the cottage... but heading straight for the dunes. Catherine stood still. Mike motioned for her to stay where she was. She watched him climb the dunes, his eyes holding hers, mesmerising her, making her heart spin crazily across her chest, up to her throat, down to her stomach and up again to explode in her eyes.

Her mind whirled with a million thoughts. Why wasn't he on his way to Sydney? Had he decided against the trip? Could... could he not bear to leave her? Was that it? Could it possibly be?

He had reached the top. He stood directly in front of her, the breeze flicking back his black hair, the moon behind him casting dark shadows across his hard cheeks. He hadn't changed, she saw. He was still wearing a white shirt but the maroon tie was loosened at his neck. The wind pressed the fabric of his grey trousers against the hard muscular contours of his thighs. He spoke, his teeth an even gleam of startling whiteness against the full cut of his darkly sensuous lips.

'I didn't get a chance to tell you,' he began, his voice blocking out the wind and the sound of the sea and filling her ears with only the sound of him. 'I'm leaving for Sydney this evening... soon.'

Catherine nodded. 'I know. I...I heard you tell the others.'

'I meant to tell you, too.' His shoulders lifted slightly in an almost helpless shrug. 'That business with the candles...Lucy...' He sighed deeply and the moonlight caught the anger in his eyes. 'I must again apologise for my daughter's behaviour.'

'Don't be upset,' Catherine said softly and it was all she could do to keep from reaching out to him, to smooth away the weariness she saw etched in his face, to press her lips against his eyelids and rid him of his despair. Instead, she added softly. 'I've had my share of apologising for my own daughter. In fact, sometimes I think apologising is one of the things parents often learn to do best.'

'Perhaps, you're right. And Jessie? How is she?'

'She's fine. We lit more candles.'

A deep, dark flush stained his cheeks and Catherine saw a flash of anger sweep once more across his eyes. She added quickly, wisely changing the subject. 'I thought you would have been gone. I heard you say you were taking an early flight. It must be close to nine by now.'

He glanced briefly at his watch. 'Closer to ten.'

Her eyes widened. 'Really? I...I came up here a little after eight. I...I can't believe I've been here for almost two hours.'

'It's a good place to be.' He looked out at the ocean, his hands shoved into the pockets of his trousers, the wind buffeting his hair, his expression revealing nothing...nothing that she could see, that she could actually describe, though it affected her deeply all the same. He continued to look out at the ocean, his eyes seemingly locked to something visible only to him.

Catherine stood perfectly still, her eyes fixed on his rugged profile, hardly daring to breathe lest she disturb him while wondering painfully if he had forgotten she was even there.

He turned slowly to look at her, saw she was watching him, and a softness entered his eyes. 'You seemed surprised to see me.'

'I was. I...I thought you had already gone.'

'Without first saying goodbye?'

She nodded. 'Yes.'

He came closer to her. His intoxicating scent blended with the crisp salt air and she breathed deeply while unaware that she was breathing at all.

'And...did that upset you?'

She gazed helplessly into his eyes. 'Yes,' she whispered, her voice barely heard above the wind but heard clearly by him. His eyes narrowed, almost as if he didn't wish fully to see what was contained in her own.

'Why?' he demanded harshly. 'Was it because you thought I was being deliberately rude and insensitive?' He paused, then added flatly, 'Prominent Donahue traits?'

'No, of course not.'

'What, then?' His hands snaked out and gripped her bare shoulders, the silky skin warm and soft beneath his touch. 'Tell me,' he demanded hoarsely.

Catherine felt her throat tightening and when she spoke her voice was uneven. 'I was upset because...because I wanted to say goodbye and...and to wish you a safe trip and to tell you...' Her voice trailed off and she bit her bottom lip while her eyes continued to gaze helplessly into his. She had almost added what she dared not. To tell him she would miss him and would be thinking about him.

His hands tightened on her slender shoulders and his eyes bored mercilessly into hers. 'What else?' He searched her face. 'You were about to say something else.'

'I was about to say that...'

'Yes?'

'That I hoped... your business dealings would go well.'

His breath left him in a shuddering sigh and his hands shook on her shoulders before leaving them altogether. He turned to gaze once more towards the turbulent sea, his expression hard and unmoving. Catherine watched him, her heart sick with despair. Before he had turned so abruptly away from her she had witnessed something in his eyes, something which made her wish she had told him the truth.

The wind picked up the hem of her dress and swirled it high above her knees. The yellow scarf billowed about her head and she felt her hair coming loose. She lifted her hands to tighten the sash but his voice stopped her.

'Leave it!' His eyes roamed the seas. 'Let your hair free.'

Catherine paused, her slender arms raised behind her head, the dress moulding itself around the curves of her nubile body, and the effect was provocative, made even more so because it was totally innocent. Mike turned slowly to look at her, his deep, dark eyes penetrating hers before drifting slowly down the length of her body, fanning the flames which scorched her being.

He walked towards her, slowly, and with each step he took the roar grew louder in her ears, louder than any waves crashing on the shore beneath them. Her arms were still raised behind her head and she felt her breasts push against the fabric of her dress, shamelessly begging for his touch. His eyes were molten pools of passion and she felt herself sinking, drowning in their depths. He reached for her hands and lowered them to her sides, his eyes never leaving her own. She felt his hands on her hair, the sash slipping away, his long, strong fingers moving through the silken tresses and lightly touching the delicate skin of her nape. Catherine shivered and her bottom lip trembled; he lowered his dark head and took it in his mouth, biting down on it gently, and when she trembled again he bit a little harder and a little harder, until she was whimpering and straining against him, pushing her aching breasts against his massive chest, the tender erect tips burning against his own heat, her hands clutching at his back, her nails digging into his hard flesh, their thighs pressed together, the throbbing, pulsing spear of his manhood a burning wedge between them. His mouth covered hers and she opened wide her own and he impaled her with his tongue, driving it deep, thrusting it to the back of her throat, filling her, and still she wanted more. His hands moved down to the rounded curves of her bottom, and he pulled her up against him, grinding her into him, and her breath came with his, fast and deep. He reached up, pushed aside the strap of her dress and freed her breast. The fiery tip was a startling red, jutting up from the perfect white mound. He teased it with his tongue, pulled on it, sucked on it, drawing it in and out of his mouth, his huge hand cupping it, guiding it, imprisoning it, torturing it with exquisite pain while his other hand remained below, curved around her bottom. Finally he released her breast, kissed it gently, almost soothingly, before pulling down her other strap. The rounded white breast looked innocent and vulnerable...until the strong brown fingers stroked it and his mouth came down to claim it.

Catherine cried out with sheer physical agony when the exquisite torture stopped. Her hazel eyes were drugged, glazed black with passion. His hands were on her shoulders, firmly holding her away. She stared at him, still in her other world, totally uncomprehending the one he was forcing back on her. She swayed uncertainly and he steadied her, his hands firmly gripping her small shoulders, almost black against her fragile whiteness. Her breasts were still exposed, glowing like the smoothest satin under the pale moonlight, the tips swollen and bruised, fulfilled. Mike released her, ran the backs of his hands gently across them, and just as gently pulled up the straps of her dress and covered her. Catherine remained motionless, her cheeks flushed, her rosy lips parted and he pressed his mouth to them and she felt his strong warm arms going around her, gathering her close, his hand stroking her hair. She closed her eyes and her own arms encircled his waist as she laid her cheek against his chest and listened to the pounding beat of his heart. Tears burned at the back of her lids and she didn't know why this should be happening; she squeezed her eyes tighter still, but still they burned.

He walked with her to the edge of the dunes, his arm warm around her slender shoulders, and she knew he would soon be leaving, that he would say goodbye, and she didn't want to cry and make a scene but she knew she would feel terribly cold when he took his arm away. She told herself that it was only for ten days and then he would be back and...and she would feel warm again.

Mike held her hand as he guided her down the steep bank of the sand dune. Neither spoke. They reached the Jaguar. He opened the door. A light came on. She saw his jacket folded across the back of the passenger seat, a bulging black leather briefcase on the floor, his car keys dangling from the ignition. He stood with one hand on the door, his eyes on her face. The wind scattered her hair and she felt it around her cheeks. He reached behind and pulled something from his hip pocket, and she saw it was her yellow sash. He gave it to her and she took it and didn't know what to do with it, and so she simply held it, a splash of yellow against the white of her dress.

'If you need anything, anything at all,' he said, his voice firm, commanding, not charged with any of the same emotions which were ripping her apart, as though he had already put behind him what had happened on the dunes, 'then I'm sure you will find it at the house. You need only ask,' he added briskly.

'Thank you,' Catherine whispered, desperately struggling to keep her raw emotions in check. His eyes darkened on her bowed head, the silky fringe of her lashes fanning her cheeks, hiding her eyes. He looked beyond her, to where the cottage stood. It stood alone, bathed in moonlight, the swaying palms rustling against the iron roof. His eyes returned to her and, when he spoke, his voice was oddly gentle but inquisitive, concerned.

'Does it worry you, being alone here?'

His caring tone unnerved her; she shook her head, not trusting herself to speak, and felt the tears flood her eyes.

'Catherine, look at me.' His hand lifted her chin and she frantically blinked her lashes but it wasn't enough. Tears sparkled like tiny jewels on the silky tips. His eyes hardened on those telltale drops and he took a deep breath, letting it out in a ragged sigh.

'It does worry you. I should have realised,' he rebuked himself. His hand moved up to cup her cheek. 'We'll get Jessie and the two of you will sleep at my place tonight. Tomorrow morning Grieves can help you move your belongings over and——'

'*No!*'

His eyes widened at her sharp retort. She backed away from him, rubbing at her cheeks with trembling fingers. 'Please! Don't...don't make us move. We...we love the cottage.'

'It's far too isolated.' His voice was factual, stern. 'There are so many strangers about this time of year. Why take risks?'

'We're not. Jessie and I have taken lessons in self-defence. We know what to do if ever we're threatened.'

'That may be, but there's always the unexpected.' He checked his watch. 'I'll get Jessie.'

'*No!*'

Mike frowned, clearly annoyed. 'I have a plane to catch. I don't have time to argue.'

He started towards the cottage, his long legs determinedly eating up the distance. Catherine hurried after him, grabbed his arm. She looked up at him with large pleading eyes. 'Please, don't. I...I wouldn't feel comfortable at your place.'

His eyes narrowed. 'Why?'

She shrugged her shoulders helplessly. How could she possibly tell him why? She was far, far too aware of him. She wouldn't be able to sleep knowing he was under the same roof. What if she did the unthinkable and crept into his room at night? She would survive the ten days he was in Sydney, but what would happen after he returned? She took a deep breath and let it out slowly. She could only imagine and her thoughts terrified her.

'I'm used to being alone. I like it—no—no, I *love* it!' She was speaking too quickly, robbing her lie of any conviction, but she wasn't aware of this, her only concern being in convincing him somehow that she mustn't in any circumstances move into the mansion...with *him*! 'If...if you make us move then...then we'll find somewhere else to stay.'

'But not at my place,' he stated coldly.

'Not at your place,' she replied unevenly, and added for emphasis, 'Most definitely not!'

A muscle worked spasmodically along his hard jaw. 'I see.' He turned abruptly back towards his car.

Catherine watched him climb into the Jag and her heart twisted painfully in her chest. She couldn't allow him to leave thinking she had been deliberately rude and ungrateful. She started towards the car. He was buckling his seatbelt but his eyes were on her, watching her slow, hesitant approach. She wanted to tell him she appreciated his concern for her and Jessie's safety and wellbeing. She wanted to tell him so many things, but how could she, when he was looking at her with ice in his frosty blue eyes?

'Have a safe trip,' she whispered huskily, and her gentle fingers touched his arm stretched across the ledge of the opened window. Something flashed briefly in his eyes and for an instant she thought she saw a bit of the ice melt in their glittering depths. But whatever it was, it was more than enough to make her lean forward and press her trembling lips against the hardness of his own. His hand reached up, touched her cheek.

'Take care,' he said gruffly.

Catherine nodded. 'You too,' she whispered, and stepped back as the powerful motor surged into life and she was left standing in the moonlight, the yellow sash still in her hand as she waved goodbye. She remained there until the tail-lights disappeared from the driveway as he turned on to the road. Only then did she make her way into the quiet loneliness of the cottage.

She poured herself a bath, stripped and sank into the relaxing warmth. Her breasts were sore, tender, and she closed her eyes and leaned back, remembering the feel of his mouth and hands and what they had done, the thrilling magic they had weaved. Ten days. Ten days was a long time. What could she possibly do to fill in the time? Physically, there were a million things, things she had been doing since forever. Taking care of Jessie, gardening, reading, housework. She could drive into Bundaberg and look at the high school she would be teaching at and browse around the shops. She could set up the beach volleyball game. That would be fun. And, of course, there was always swimming and walks along the beach, climbing the dunes and sliding back down. Yes, her days would certainly be full enough, but...but what about the nights? She squirmed uncomfortably in her bath. Don't be silly, she told herself. You love the evenings. It's your own special time, remember? That's when you do all the things you didn't get a chance to do during the day.

What special things? a taunting voice echoed in her head.

Why, you know, the first voice hedged. That's when I . . . read . . . relax . . . write letters. . . .

Pooh! You've read all your books. You've read most of them two or three times. And as for relaxing . . . well, just look at you. You're in a hot tub but you're coiled up tighter than a spring. You've got the facecloth pressed against your mouth, for goodness' sake. And what letters are we talking about here? You hardly need a correspondence secretary, the voice continued to taunt. The only letters you ever wrote were to your mother. And now you don't even have that to do. She's living right next door to you, you silly little girl! Face up to yourself, Catherine Mitchell. Your life is dull and it will continue to be for as long as you're afraid . . .

Afraid? Afraid of what? I'm *not* afraid!

Then why didn't you move over to the mansion?

You know damn well why.

Because you're *afraid!*

I'm *not!* I . . . I just didn't think it would . . . seem proper.

Proper?! Did the man ask you to become his mistress?

Catherine's cheeks burned. She pressed the facecloth tighter still against her mouth. No, of course he didn't.

Then what did he ask you?

You know perfectly well. She rolled up the facecloth into a tight little ball and drowned it.

He only asked you to move into the mansion because he was concerned for you and for Jessie. Correct

me if I'm wrong, the voice jeered, but I can't remember him asking you to move in with him specifi-
cally, just to move into the mansion.

All right! All right! So I read more into it than I
should have...

Than he intended, the voice mocked remindingly.

Than he intended, she silently agreed, and a long
sigh filled the steamy room.

So, don't you feel foolish now?

No, just....

Just what, Catherine Mitchell?

Miserable...downright miserable.

Hah! That's what I thought. Well, you have no one
to blame but yourself. I very much doubt if he will
ever offer you the same invitation again. And that's
a real shame. Who knows, he might have grown quite
attached to you...

Catherine pulled the plug from the bath with a swift
jerky movement and stepped out of the tub. She refused to listen to any more voices in her head and
towel-dried herself vigorously, practically rubbing her
skin from her body before slipping into a nightie.
There was only a slight breeze on the veranda when
she stepped outside, but the wind would be howling
on the dunes. The voices returned, to taunt and tease
her, to remind her of her cowardice and the fact that
she *had* read more into Mike's invitation than he had
ever intended. She could only hope and pray he hadn't
guessed what had driven her to refuse! Better, far, far
better for him to think she had been ungrateful...or
stubborn, or both, than to know the truth.

She started walking, the sand kicking up behind her
from her bare feet. The dunes beckoned her. She was

alone but somehow, when she was on the dunes, she never really *felt* alone. She was getting used to the steep hills, climbing them almost as expertly as Mike had done. She stood on the edge and stared down at the swirling foam-charged pools below before lifting her eyes to gaze across the endless stretch of sea. Mike had done that, stared across the vast expanse. What had he been looking at, looking for? She didn't know... any more than she knew why she was doing the very same thing.

Catherine folded her arms across her chest. It was cold up here. The wind tore at her hair and she welcomed it. *Let your hair free!* Mike's words. Mike's hands in her hair, carressing... She started to sway...slowly...moving her body back and forth the way she had against his. Was it wrong to feel this way? The wind clasped her nightie and tightened it around her long, slender legs. Still she swayed. Tears of longing rose and burned in her eyes. The wind reached out and dried them from her cheeks and she never knew they had even been there. Slowly she turned and walked away from the edge. The wind buffeted her, made her stumble. The tiny cottage rested below. Mike's cottage. She was living in Mike's cottage. And...and these were *his* dunes and she was standing on them. The ocean belonged to him too... and she swam in it. The sky was his and so was the moon... and the stars. Everything belonged to Mike. *Everything*!

Catherine slipped down the dunes, walked softly across the moon-washed beach and on to the veranda. What had she said she would do while he was away? Read, relax and write letters, wasn't it? That was what she had done, had always done, for so many years now.

She gripped the veranda rail and pressed her brow against the pillar. *It wasn't enough*! Nor ... had it ever been!

CHAPTER SEVEN

'I HATE Lucy!'

Catherine looked at Jessie and sighed. They were sitting on the veranda where Catherine was drying her hair in the full morning sun. Jessie was on the steps, elbows on her knees, chin cupped in her hands. The porcelain doll was beside her, her other gifts by her feet. Catherine knew Jessie wanted to make up with Lucy but her childish pride was standing in the way.

'You've been saying that for the past two days,' Catherine reminded her. 'I think it's time you stopped.'

'I can't help it,' Jessie muttered. 'I told you she'd spoil my party and she did! I get mad every time I think of her blowing out *my* candles.'

'You got to blow them out later.'

'But nobody got to *watch* me!'

'I did.'

'But you always watch me. I wanted Lucy to watch, and her daddy and Grandma and Albert. Instead everybody got to watch *her*!'

Catherine stood up. 'How about a game of beach volleyball?' she suggested, to get Jessie's mind off her woes.

Jessie shook her head. 'I'm sick of beach volleyball.' She glanced longingly at the game by her feet, given to her by Lucy. 'It's no fun with just you and me.'

Catherine smiled at Jessie's downcast face. 'I think you should call a truce with Lucy.'

Jessie looked up at her, horrified. 'You mean... shake hands?'

'Yup!' She sat down on the steps and drew Jessie snugly to her side. 'It seems silly, doesn't it, two little girls living so close, not speaking to each other when together they could be having lots of fun...playing with dolls...having a game of beach volleyball...' She tousled Jessie's curls. 'What do you think?'

'I don't know,' Jessie sighed. 'Maybe, if she comes over and apologises, maybe then I'll play with her.'

'What if she never comes over? What if she's feeling so badly about what she did that she thinks you don't ever want to see her again?'

Jessie relished that for a moment. 'Well, maybe I will go over there, but if Lucy doesn't apologise I'm coming straight back!' She stood up and looked at Catherine. 'Do I look all right?' she asked anxiously.

Catherine's eyes swept over her, from the top of her curling glory, down to her bright red and white striped T-shirt, denim shorts and white sneakers. 'You look absolutely perfect.' She added casually. 'Want me to go with you?'

'No,' Jessie sighed. 'I think I'd better do this on my own.'

Catherine grinned. 'Good luck!'

When Jessie returned an hour later, Catherine was busy in the garden pulling out weeds and adding them to her compost heap. 'How did it go?' she asked, knowing it must have gone extremely well judging from the look on Jessie's face.

'Well, Mrs Beasley said I couldn't see Lucy, that *I* was always getting *Lucy* into trouble. Can you *believe* that?' Jessie added scornfully.

Coming from Mrs Beasley, Catherine could believe it all right. She frowned. 'So you didn't see Lucy? Why have you been gone so——?'

'I *did* see her!' Jessie's eyes glowed with mischief. 'I snuk around to the back and peeked in all the windows. I found Lucy sitting at a long table having lunch. She was all by herself and I felt sorry for her. She looked kinda sad and lonely. A maid came in and said if she didn't eat all her meal she wouldn't be getting any dessert. I thought Lucy would yell and scream at hearing that but she didn't. She just sat there and said nothing. When the maid left I ducked into the room. I could tell Lucy was glad to see me but she pretended she wasn't. She asked me why I had come over to see her after what she did at my party. I said I wanted to call a truce so we could play together. Lucy said Mrs Beasley would never allow that and that we would have to wait until her daddy got home but *I* said *you* would talk to Mrs Beasley and *make* her let us play together.' Jessie beamed up at Catherine. 'So will you, Mummy?'

Catherine sighed. 'Well, I suppose I could have a chat with her, but I don't think I can *make* her!'

'But you will try?' Jessie pleaded.

'Yes, I'll at least do that.'

Catherine and Jessie paid a visit to Mrs Beasley later that day. At first Mrs Beasley refused to listen to any such proposal. 'I'm responsible for the child when her father is away,' she stated in her cold, imperious manner. 'I can't have her running back and forth along the beach or through the wood not knowing where she is or when she will be back. We're expecting a house full of guests soon and I'm very busy getting ready for them. I haven't time to chase after the child.'

But eventually a compromise was reached. Lucy was made to promise she would never go over to Dune Cottage while her father wasn't home and Jessie was made to promise she would never set foot on the mansion's step before ten o'clock in the morning and that she would leave promptly at three in order that Lucy could have afternoon tea with her grandfather before practising her piano. The girls cheerfully agreed to all conditions and hailed Catherine as their heroine.

With Jessie at the mansion for the better part of each day, Catherine was left to her own devices. She drove into Bundaberg, walked around the school she would be teaching at and visited a few estate agencies to check on the availability of flats and the rents she would be expected to pay. Afterwards she had lunch at a gracious park overlooking the Burnett River, meandering its way through the pretty coastal sugar-town. She thought constantly of Mike, wondering what he might be doing at this or that very minute, and wondering too if he ever thought of her and what she might be doing.

She went for long walks, exploring the countryside behind the little cottage, following treks and overgrown paths which usually led nowhere. On one such day she found a treasure! Deep in the hills behind the cottage she heard the sound of rushing water. She followed the sound and entered a thick tropical jungle, similar to a rainforest with lush green foliage. There was a moss-covered clearing, cool and deeply shaded with towering ferns overhanging a series of rock pools.

Water cascaded down a glistening wall, filling the pools to overflowing, the water pouring into the one below and the one below that. The water was crystal-clear and when she knelt and felt it it was icy cold. It was all so peaceful, so utterly beautiful that Catherine was reluctant to leave. She stayed an hour and then hurried back to the cottage to be there for when Jessie returned.

The next day she returned and brought a small picnic lunch. She swam naked in the clear water, basked on the spongy moss and left feeling totally refreshed. It became *her* place. She didn't tell Jessie about her discovery in case Jessie might wander there alone. The pools were deep and dangerous.

The day before Mike was due home, Catherine dropped Jessie off to play with Lucy and continued on to the village. She parked the MG in front of the sporting goods shop and saw the tall blond young man she had spoken to earlier about the bikes...when Mike had so abruptly brought a halt to her enquiries. She gave him a brief wave as she alighted from the car. He walked over to her.

'Thought any more about having a spin on one of the bikes?' he asked her with a friendly smile, his eyes sweeping over her in an appreciative glance. She was wearing thigh-length pastel green shorts and a darker green sleeveless T-shirt. Her hair was pulled back and held with a russet-coloured scarf.

She hadn't, but didn't want to offend him by so admitting. 'I don't know,' she hedged. 'It looks ... rather dangerous, as though the bikes would wobble.'

He tossed her a grin. 'Only one way to find out.' He pulled out one of the bikes from a rack. 'And that's to have a go.'

Catherine hesitated, knowing her reluctance was caused by the fact Mike hadn't approved of her speaking with the young man earlier.

'The shop isn't busy at the moment; at least nothing my assistant can't handle. We'll go for a ride and you can decide for yourself if it's dangerous or not.' He brought the bike over to her. 'My name is Wade Curtis. I'd really like to know your name.'

'Catherine Mitchell.' She grinned. 'All right. I'll give it a try.'

Catherine mounted one of the bikes and Wade the other. They didn't wobble and it was fun. They kept to the footpath until Catherine felt confident enough to go out on to the road. They picked up speed. Her brightly coloured scarf blew in the breeze. She felt carefree and just a little reckless. 'This is great!' she shouted to Wade, her face bright with laughter as they rounded a sharp bend in the road.

There was a screech of brakes and the bikes teetered dangerously before Wade managed to get them under control and to a halt beside the road. Catherine stared at a silver-grey Jaguar as it came to a shuddering stop just ahead. She caught Mike's eyes in the rear-view mirror and his glaring anger left her shaken. He started up the motor and roared around the bend, disappearing in a cloud of dust.

'Whew!' Wade exclaimed. 'That was close!'

They rode back to the shop in a subdued silence. Catherine was shaken but not entirely from the near miss with the Jaguar. Mike's eyes boring into her own had unsettled her far more, even though she realised that if he hadn't been such a skilful driver she and Wade might have been badly injured.

However, by the time she had purchased her groceries and returned to the cottage all she could think about was that Mike was home! Her whole being was flooded with happiness and she was very much aware of an excited anticipation in the pit of her stomach. Would he come over to see her? Tell her about his trip? She hurriedly put away the groceries, tidied her hair and freshened herself up with a quick wash. She was sitting on the veranda with a glass of cold lemonade in her hands, thinking about him, when a shadow fell over her.

A delighted smile swept across her face and she lifted her hand to shield her eyes from the sun in order to see him better. He was home a day earlier than planned and he had come over to see her. Her heart swelled in her chest.

But now that she could see him better, she could also see the black scowl on his face and the dark anger blazing in his eyes. Her heart sank. She rose slowly to her feet, her welcoming smile freezing on her lips. 'Mike,' she said stiffly. 'I'm so glad...'

He climbed the few steps, removed the glass from her trembling fingers and placed it with a sharp bang on the cane table beside the chair she had been sitting upon. His eyes lashed her with the fury of a thousand whips.

'And what have you been up to since I've been away?' he asked in a deadly cold voice.

Catherine hesitated. She had planned to tell him all about her days, especially about the beautiful rock pools she had found where maybe, when he wasn't too busy, they could take a picnic. But she knew he wouldn't be interested...not in his present dark mood.

'Not much,' she answered with a sigh.

'*Not much*?' he exploded, and his hands shot out and grabbed her shoulders, his hard fingers piercing her tender flesh like burning coals. 'It certainly didn't look that way to me!'

He meant the bike, of course. His next words confirmed it. 'Of all the irresponsible stunts!' he rasped. 'Riding like a couple of dim-witted children on a road barely wide enough for a car to pass.' He gave her a shake. 'Have you no sense of responsibility whatsoever?'

'Of course I have.' She winced as his fingers dug deeper, the coals burning hotter. 'I...I was *testing* the bike...to see if it was s-safe and...and it was fun and...'

'*Fun!*' he exploded. 'You could have been *killed!*' Catherine started to protest but he shook her into a shuddering silence. 'Had it been someone with less experience than myself you could be fighting for your life right now, and you call that *fun?*'

Anger rose within her, swift and sharp. 'Well, if *you* hadn't been driving as if the road belonged to you alone there wouldn't have been an accident in the first place!'

'And if you had been here where you belong, looking after your child instead of turning that responsibility over to Mrs Beasley, we wouldn't be having this discussion!' he lashed back.

'Discussion?' she flared. 'This isn't a discussion, this is an *outrage!*' She shook herself free of his vice-like grip. 'How dare you insinuate I've been neglecting my child?'

'Insinuate? Hell, woman, I was stating a *fact!*'

Her eyes narrowed. 'Well, here's a fact for you. *My* child never has to sit alone to eat her meals. *My* child...'

Catherine stopped short. Good grief, what was she doing...saying? Mike looked as if he had suddenly been struck in the face. His broad shoulders heaved and he drew in a quick breath.

'I...I'm sorry,' she whispered, gazing helplessly up at him. 'I didn't mean to get personal.'

But her remark only seemed to infuriate him more. The bleakness she had seen dispersed before her very eyes. He drew himself up, tall and angry, and she felt her own temper rising again in response. It became a silent battle of their wills. Mike broke the tense, bristling hush.

'I rarely take personally irrational comments,' he stated frostily, 'but I do object strongly to my staff being taken advantage of, and apparently that's what you've been doing!'

The idea of her taking advantage of his staff was so ludicrous that she could only stare at him in absolute bewilderment. 'How?'

'I've already told you,' he stated derisively. 'As much as it pleases me that Lucy has found a friend in Jessie, it doesn't please me that you've allowed your child to spend practically every waking moment under the care of Mrs Beasley while you engage in reckless activities and...' His eyes hardened. 'And God knows what else!'

It was the "God knows what else!" that really got to her and was responsible for the angry flush which steamed her cheeks. 'Mrs Beasley will only allow the girls to play together between ten and three and *only* at your house! *Her* stipulations...*her* rules, not *mine*!'

Suddenly Catherine felt the fight going out of her. Maybe it was the way Mike was looking at her, with his unfathomable deep blue eyes which had the ability to probe into her very soul while shutting her out of his own. Maybe it was the hurt she felt as she struggled with her emotions. She had so looked forward to seeing him again, to hearing his voice, to being near him, with him. But now she realised she had been fantasising. Mike Donahue wasn't interested in sharing any part of his life with her. His only concern was that no one interfered with the smooth-running operations of his domestic life.

'I can see now,' she stated, her voice cloaked in pain, 'that I should never have allowed Jessie to go over to your place. I . . . I didn't realise it would cause so much trouble.' Her throat felt raw as she added. 'Please, when you get back, please send her home.'

'Nonsense!' He drew in his breath and let it out slowly. 'The trouble hasn't been with Jessie and you damn well know it!'

Catherine waited for him to say more. His jaw clenched and unclenched but he remained silent. For a moment they simply stared at each other, their eyes braked in collision, neither prepared to give in. Infuriated, Mike turned on his heel and stalked down the steps.

'When are you going to take time out from your . . . *fun* . . . and see about these tyres?' he roared as he came to an abrupt halt beside her car.

Catherine came up to him, her arms folded protectively across her chest. 'What's wrong with them?' she asked stiffly.

'What's wrong with them?' he repeated as if he had never before heard such a dumb question. 'They're bald!'

'They are not. They're retreads. I've only had them for three months.' She added disdainfully. 'It's not enough to pick on *me*, now you have to pick on my *car*!'

'Don't be ridiculous!' he snarled and bent to more thoroughly examine the rubber, passing an expert hand over the smooth exterior. 'I'm amazed you haven't been pulled over by the police. These tyres are worn thin . . . *bald*!'

She touched her hair. 'Thank goodness *I'm* not or you'd want to get rid of my head!'

He slowly straightened to his full height. 'Don't give me ideas!'

It was all too much for Catherine. She wanted to kick him, lash out at him in some painful manner, hurt him the way his words had hurt her. She stepped closer to him, bristling with her fury. Close enough to smell his aftershave and his intoxicating male scent. Close enough to see the fine, silky black hairs curling lightly between the V of his opened neck shirt. Close enough to pummel her small fists against his broad chest and close enough for him to grab those fists and whip them smartly behind her back, pinning her against him while his smouldering blue eyes held her . . . trapped.

And it was then she knew. Knew she could never hurt him. She could only . . . *love him*!

Love him! Her eyes widened as she stared up at him. She felt the angry tension drain from her body and a far more disturbing tension filling it, flooding her with a startling new awareness. But was it so new?

Shock ripped through her as she realised it wasn't. Hadn't been for a very long time. How long? A picture flashed into her shattered brain. A picture of herself, sitting on the veranda the night he had found the pail and placed it by the door. She had given herself to him then just as surely as if she had reached inside her and handed him her heart. And earlier...earlier, when she had performed that crazy dance on the dunes... She had felt something then, could feel it still, had never forgotten it, that gripping sensation of not being alone. He had arrived at the mansion almost the same time she had arrived at the cottage. Her mother had told her that, and she had seen him in the Jaguar. He had always been there, here, in her heart! She *loved* him! Oh, dear God, how she loved him!

Now she finally understood why she had felt so desolate the night he left for Sydney. Why she had felt the need to climb the dunes, not once but twice. It was to be with him again. To feel, somehow, his presence.

She continued to stare up at him, her beautiful hazel eyes wide, startled, frightened as a doe's gazing helplessly up at the hunter, his eyes like a double barrelled shotgun aiming straight at her. Her body trembled against him, her breasts tingling against his hard chest. Her hands were still imprisoned behind her, one huge hand holding them there while his free hand slowly encircled her neck, his long fingers spreading through her hair, the hard gleam in his eyes glittering down at her, and she was powerless to look away. She watched, hypnotised, as his head slowly descended, his mouth so close she could almost taste him. Her breath caught in her throat. She couldn't breathe. She

was actually suffocating. Never had his eyes seemed
so cruel. A small, strangled cry tore from her throat.
His mouth hovered above hers, a bee about to take
his honey from the soft, trembling petals of the
sweetest flower. She felt herself moving closer, the
lower part of her body straining shamelessly against
him, the heat between her thighs moving over her,
through her, into her, and he felt it and his eyes grew
crueller still.

'Kiss me!' he ordered, and she obeyed. Her lips
touched his, a mere whisper of a touch, but the results
were explosive, shattering. With a strangled cry he released her hands and pulled her even closer against
him, their bodies straining against each other, their
mouths bruising and punishing, their hands searching,
exploring...

And she was as helpless as the tides against the force
of the moon.

CHAPTER EIGHT

THIRTY degrees in the shade and there she was...
mowing the lawn! Mike shook his head. He had never
known a woman so damnably independent.

He stood on the dunes and continued to watch her,
marvelling at the skilful manner in which she ma-
noeuvred the old mower. He would instruct Grieves
to find her something better, something easier to op-
erate. He hadn't meant to walk this far. He had only
wanted to get away from the house for a few moments, spend some time alone. Ordinarily he enjoyed
this planned once-a-year get-together with colleagues
and friends, but this time he felt oddly detached from
them, almost like a stranger among his own people.

Below him, Catherine removed the catcher from the
mower and tipped the clippings on to her compost
heap, then turned around to survey the lawn. She
picked up a few errant twigs and leaves and tossed
them on to the heap. She knew he was there. She had
known the moment his head had appeared over the
dunes. A rush of warmth followed by a burst of happiness had exploded within her. She had taken several
peeks at him. How tall and magnificent he looked,
silhouetted against the pale blue sky like a proud
Greek god.

Catherine hadn't spoken to him since his guests had
arrived but that hadn't kept her from thinking about
him. Constantly. She hadn't realised that one person

could so completely dominate another person's
thoughts . . . invade their dreams.

Even while mowing the lawn she had been thinking
about him, wondering about his guests and one guest
in particular. Her mother had told her about Renata,
the beautiful blonde model, who hardly ever left his
side.

But Renata wasn't with him now. He was alone.
And obviously he had come to see her. Why else would
he be up there, looking down at her? If only she had
started the lawn earlier she could have showered and
changed out of her denim shorts and old blue shirt.
Her Greek god looked so fresh in his pale grey trousers
and white shirt, the sleeves rolled up his tanned forearms and the soft, hot breeze tossing back his thick
black hair. The mere sight of him was a feast for her
love-starved heart.

It was time now to acknowledge his presence, let
him know she had seen him. She picked up one last
twig and as she tossed it on to the heap she looked
up at him, her arm continuing in a wave, a bright
smile on her lips. The smile froze and her arm dropped
like a lifeless thing. Mike wasn't watching her. He was
helping someone on to the dunes. Someone with long
blonde hair and a voluptuous body wrapped tightly
in a bright blue sarong. The blonde was laughing and
she flung herself into his arms, her leg kicking up
provocatively as she kissed him fully on the mouth.

Catherine stared in stunned, morbid fascination
until scalding tears burned her eyes and she could see
no more. She turned and fled blindly into the cottage,
a dreadful nausea spreading in the pit of her stomach.
Mike hadn't been on the dunes to see her. He had
been waiting for Renata; a few planned stolen mo-

ments together away from their friends. What a fool she had been to think otherwise.

And added to her hurt, her anguish, was the humiliation of knowing she had been showing off for him. Mowing the grass with such care, picking up leaves and twigs as if she would allow nothing at all to mar his lawn and tossing them so gracefully on to the compost heap as if they were dainty little feathers and she a ballerina. How silly she must have looked; how utterly ridiculous, especially in this blistering heat. And while she had mowed and fussed, dressed like a farmer's daughter, he had merely been waiting for his gorgeous blonde, a woman who obviously knew of better ways to entertain her man.

Catherine pulled her hands from her burning face and her anguished eyes stared straight ahead at the little Christmas tree she and Jessie had decorated last evening. Jessie was over at the mansion playing with Lucy and the children belonging to Mike's guests. She would be back soon and it wouldn't do to find Mummy with red eyes and tears rolling down her cheeks. She went into the bathroom and stripped herself bare. The cold water pelting down from the shower cooled her but did nothing to alleviate her misery.

She had listened to her mother's accounts about Mike and his guests and had pretended to be greatly amused by their antics, but it had only made her miss him more. Betty had told her about their dancing in the ballroom and on the poolside terrace. She had told her about the midnight clam-bakes, the sailing, swimming and games. And Catherine could have joined them had she wished. She had certainly been invited often enough. Whenever Mike learned that

Betty was on her way over, he always said to tell Catherine that this or that was about to happen and she was welcome to join them. But she never did. Partly out of shyness, but mainly because she felt if Mike really wanted her he would have asked her himself. She was convinced he had invited her only out of courtesy.

Catherine stepped out of the shower and, without drying herself off, slipped into her pale blue cotton robe. The heat struck her as soon as she entered the lounge.

'Enjoy your shower?' The deep-timbred voice came from the dusky shadows of the corner of the lounge. Catherine's eyes widened as Mike slowly rose from a chair, a magazine held loosely in his hand. Her heart thumped loudly in her ears and her throat felt suddenly dry. She struggled to keep an iron control of her emotions as her eyes swept the room, half expecting to find Renata draped in one of the chairs. But the room was empty...except for the two of them. *The two of them*!

'Why...why are you here?' Her voice trembled in the stillness of the room.

'To see you.' And he couldn't tear his eyes from the picture she made, standing there, her cotton robe clinging to her damp skin, outlining the sensuous curves of thighs and hips, her erect nipples pushing invitingly against the thin fabric and her hair tumbling to her slender shoulders in a glorious and wild abandonment. His eyes rested seductively on hers and she saw the blatant invitation in those smouldering satanic orbs.

Anger rose like bile in her throat. How dared he look at her like *that* after having been with Renata?

She couldn't believe he could be so insensitive, so uncaring. Hurt mingled with the anger in her eyes and she tightened the sash of her robe.

'Why did you want to see me?' she asked as coolly as her poor tormented soul would allow, while she wrestled with her emotions, wanting him to go, wanting him to stay—desperately wanting him to stay—despising herself for her weakness and despising *him* because he was the cause of it. 'If...if it's about Jessie spending so...so much time at your——'

'It's not about Jessie. I just wanted to see you.' His eyes probed her face. 'Is something wrong?'

'Wrong?' she repeated. Her eyes glowed with a burning brightness. 'What could possibly be wrong?'

'Something's troubling you.' He moved up to her and gently pushed back the tumbled mass of dampened hair from her flushed cheeks. She closed her eyes as a painful sob rose in her throat. Frantically she swallowed it but another one threatened. Why was he doing this to her? Why was he pretending to be so caring?

'Something is definitely troubling you,' he stated gruffly, and his fingers lightly touched her trembling lips. 'Tell me what it is.'

Catherine pushed his hand away. 'Nothing is troubling me. You...you startled me, that's all. I...I didn't know you were here.' Her voice was choked. 'How dare you simply walk in uninvited? Perhaps I should be paying you rent? In fact, I insist upon it. That way you won't have the right to barge in whenever it takes your fancy!'

She glared at him as if barging in on her was something he liked doing best and often! His eyes lost their concern and became cold, like shards of ice.

'There's not a chance I'd ever charge you rent,' he lashed back. 'To do so would give you certain rights. I wouldn't be allowed to evict you at a moment's notice.' He added with cutting cruelty, 'When I've had enough of you!'

'Enough of me?' she repeated, her voice charged with emotion. 'You will never have enough of me, Mike Donahue. You will never have me at all!'

Catherine caught her breath, wishing she had held her tongue. His eyes gleamed with dangerous lights.

'You're a beautiful and desirable woman, Catherine Mitchell,' he drawled seductively, 'and you were right when you said I could never have enough of you.' Hot colour rose high on her cheeks as he added, 'But you were wrong when you said I would never have you at all!'

The silence was electrifying. Fire and flame touched her, scorched her. She could actually feel her breasts swell and push against her robe. The magnetism between them was undeniable. His eyes held hers with a fierce intensity as he reached out for her, his hand encircling her waist, pulling her against him, his other hand untying her sash and slipping her robe from her slender shoulders and down her arms. Catherine felt it brush against her fevered skin as it fell to the floor.

She stood naked before him, her head tilted slightly back, a proud defiance blazing in her eyes while the blood pounded in her brain and exploded from her heart. Her knees trembled as his mouth covered hers, his hands cupping her breasts, and he pushed his tongue hard into her mouth and she bit down on it, greedily, her hands moving up to dig her fingers into his scalp, reveling in the feel of the coarse texture of his hair. She returned his kisses with a ravishing hunger which quite matched his own.

They weren't gentle with each other. Neither wanted that. His hands were bruising as they explored her body, his mouth leaving a trail of quivering flesh as his lips touched her in places which left her gasping. He drew her throbbing nipples into his mouth, punishing each one exquisitely with his teeth before soothing it with his tongue. His hand moved down the silky curves of her body, across her stomach and between the moist heat of her thighs, stroking the core of her womanhood. Long, shuddering moans of erotic pleasure tore from her throat. She couldn't stop them, nor could she disguise them. They burst from her heart; a heart consumed with the love and the anguish she felt for this man.

When her shudderings gradually ceased, he pulled her against him, his hands gentle now as he smoothed back her hair from her fevered cheeks, and she laid her face against his chest. She could feel the silky black hairs damp against his tanned skin. She couldn't remember unbuttoning his shirt but knew she must have. What else had she done? Her cheeks burned as she remembered. But she knew she could never do enough for him, this man whom she loved like no other. She moved slightly in his arms to gaze lovingly up at him and to touch his cheek and his lips, as gentle with him now as he was with her.

'I love you!' she whispered, and it was a cry wrenched from her heart, filled with the emotion that consumed her being. 'I love you so much!'

She felt him stiffen. It was as if he had mysteriously built a wall between their bodies, their hearts, an invisible barrier that couldn't be penetrated. She felt suddenly cold, sickened, and she shivered and pulled away from him. He picked up her robe and helped her into it, tying the sash around her waist, and she pretended that nothing was wrong, that her heart hadn't been smashed into a million pieces, that he hadn't heard those three little words when she knew he had.

She watched him do up the buttons of his shirt, his long, tanned fingers dark against the white. He didn't smile at her, no attractive male dimples forming deep grooves in his handsome face. Did Renata like his dimples? she tortured herself further by wondering, and knew that of course she would. What woman wouldn't.

'Why haven't you accepted any of my invitations to join me and my guests?' he asked as he tucked his shirt into his trousers, his tone light, casual, and she knew he was only making small talk while he made himself presentable before returning to his friends...to *her*.

'Perhaps I would have,' she answered stiffly, 'had you asked me.'

'But I asked you many times.'

'I meant...personally.' She wished he would leave. She desperately needed to be alone, to analyse what had happened between them...and, more importantly, what she might have done to avoid it.

He chuckled, those male dimples finally doing their thing. 'Since when have you ever needed a personal invitation to do whatever you wished?' he drawled, his voice light with teasing humour. She tried to smile, to join into his light-heartedness, to continue her pretence that nothing was wrong, that she hadn't been mortally wounded, but her lips refused to obey.

But she needn't have bothered. He continued in that same light-hearted tone. 'They were only impromptu happenings, nothing formal.' He cupped her chin in his hand and gently raised it. She looked steadily up at him, her eyes huge in her pale face. He kissed the tip of her nose. 'How do you like live theatre?'

'I . . . I love it.'

'Good!' The corners of his eyes crinkled in a shimmering haze of blue as he smiled down at her upturned face. 'I've booked the best seats in the house at the Moncrieffe for the lot of us.' His smile deepened. 'Consider yourself formally invited.

Her face grew paler. 'When?'

'Saturday night. I'll pick you up at eight. Jessie can stay with Lucy and the other children. We'll have supper afterwards, maybe a swim if this heat keeps up.'

'I . . . I can't.' Her voice sounded tragic.

Mike frowned. '*Can't*?' He repeated the word as if he had never heard it before.

'I . . . I already have a date . . . for the theatre . . . for Saturday night.'

'Break it!'

He stated the words casually, as if there was really no problem, of course she would break her date in order to be with him. And why wouldn't he think that? Catherine wondered with growing despair. Hadn't she just been in his arms? Hadn't she just told him she loved him? He probably considered her now as merely one of his many possessions. He would beckon...she would crawl. He would command . . . she would obey.

She had seen him in action before, knew the power he yielded over people. And yet, for all that, she desperately wanted to obey. She would willingly become his slave, obey his every command . . . if only he loved her the way she loved him.

She shook her head. 'I can't.'

'You keep saying that!' Anger sharpened his voice. 'Why can't you?'

He didn't understand. She lowered her eyes, her heart aching. 'Because I was asked over a week ago . . . and I said yes . . . and the tickets have already been bought and . . . and because I didn't know you . . . *you* would be inviting me.'

Her sad and lonely eyes looked up at him when he didn't immediately speak. His face was dark with anger and blue flames ignited his eyes. She knew what it was costing him to keep his control. Mike Donahue didn't take kindly to being thwarted in any way, even if it was only over a simple thing, like refusing an invitation.

'Who asked you?' he demanded harshly.

Her emotions backfired and veered sharply towards anger at his tone. 'I don't think that is any of your business,' she replied quietly.

It was the wrong thing to say. She had given him the excuse he had been seeking to vent his full wrath. His hands shot out and gripped her shoulders.

'Of course it's my business!' he exploded, his voice seething with rage. 'You're my guest, my responsibility! It's my right, my *duty*, to know where you go and with *whom*!'

'You have no hold over me!' Catherine lashed back, hot tears stinging her eyes. 'But if you must know, I'm going with Wade Curtis.'

'Wade Curtis?' he repeated, the name rolling off his lips with obvious distaste. 'Who is *that*?'

This was the part she had been dreading...had hoped to avoid. 'He...he's the owner of that sporting goods shop in the village,' she mumbled.

Mike's eyes widened with fresh outrage. He shook her. '*Him*? You're going with *him*? The *idiot* who almost got you *killed*?'

Flames of righteous indignation scorched her cheeks. 'He's very nice and...'

Mike dropped his hands from her shoulders and jammed them into the pockets of his trousers. He gazed down at her as if she were a delinquent child in need of his protection. 'All right, accept the date if you must, but I want both of you to join my group. I'll pick you up first then we can drive around to fetch...'

Catherine stared up at him with round, incredulous eyes. 'Good grief!' she exploded. 'We're not teenagers in need of a chaperon. We'll go on our own, thank you very much!' She added stiffly. 'I couldn't imagine anything worse than spending an entire evening under your reproachful eyes!'

They glared at each other, their eyes gripped in open combat, their unspoken thoughts sizzling between them with startling ferocity.

'Well,' Mike snarled. 'Enjoy the show, Mrs Mitchell!'

'I certainly intend to, Mr Donahue!'

And she watched him go, his long angry strides taking him across the hot white sands. His back was stiff, taut with the emotions which clenched his muscles, tightened his spine. He climbed the dunes and disappeared down the other side. It was only then that Catherine relaxed her own stiff control, and when she did she felt limp, exhausted, as if she had indeed been in a battle. The searing heat swept up from the sands, hitting her like blasts from a furnace, but she shivered as if from cold. She turned from the doorway and entered the lounge, and suddenly a most wondrous thought struck her. Her face lit up, her smile radiant. Mike had asked her out! For a date! Certainly that had to mean *something*! Unfortunately she wouldn't be able to actually sit beside him at the theatre, but she would know he was there. In her heart she would *pretend* that she was with him, next to him, and—well, that would have to be enough. Her smile grew more radiant still. At least for now!

CHAPTER NINE

CATHERINE looked down at Jessie's face. The child was flushed with excitement and her eyes were shining. They were also pleading.

'May I, Mummy, please?' she begged. 'All the other children are going and it will be so much fun!'

'But, darling, we'd planned to go on Sunday. Don't you remember?'

'I know and I told Lucy's daddy that, but he said weekends were the worst possible times to go and that it would be so crowded we wouldn't get anywhere near to the turtles to see them lay their eggs.' She grabbed Catherine's hand. 'Please let me go, Mummy. It will be so much fun with Lucy and all the other kids.'

Catherine bit back her disappointment. Disappointment made all the more potent because it was flooded with hurt. Why hadn't Mike included her in the invitation...especially when Jessie had told him *she* had planned to take her to view the great loggerhead turtles at Mon Repos beach on Sunday. He would have had to realise he was interfering with her plans, spoiling an outing she had been looking forward to, and she couldn't help wondering if he hadn't done it deliberately to...to punish her for refusing his invitation to the theatre.

'All right, Jessie,' she sighed. 'You may go. When...when is he picking you up?'

'In an hour and I'm to be ready. It will get dark while we're there so I'm to take along a sweater just

113

in case it cools down.' She added importantly, 'We'll be back late.'

'But what about your dinner?' Catherine turned to look at the stove where a pot of chicken stew was starting to bubble, a stew she had taken the time to prepare despite the heat. 'Am I expected to keep that warm for you?' she added crossly.

Jessie looked at her mother in surprise. 'Are you angry with me, Mummy? Don't...don't you want me to go?'

'I'm sorry, darling. I didn't mean to snap at you like that. I guess it's the heat.' Her hand shook as she turned off the stove. 'We can have this tomorrow night. I'll fix you some toasted cheese sandwiches when you get back.' She added with a sigh. 'Hadn't you better get ready? You don't want to keep everyone waiting.'

Catherine watched Jessie as she scampered off to change out of the play outfit she had worn over to the mansion and into something a little more suitable for turtle viewing. Of course, she could have refused the child permission, and after her initial disappointment Jessie would have got over it. After all, they could go on Sunday and they would see the turtles despite Mike's claim that it would be too crowded. But she hadn't refused and she knew the reason why. She didn't want Mike thinking she held a grudge about their discussion over the theatre yesterday. She wanted him to think she had forgotten all about it.

Mike pulled up to the cottage in an impressive-looking Range Rover, packed with children. Catherine was beginning to think he owned a vehicle suitable for every occasion. Jessie gave her a quick kiss goodbye and raced out to the vehicle, thrilled to be off. But instead of the Rover leaving, the engine was switched off and Mike stepped down from it. He strolled casually towards Catherine standing by the door. A lump formed in her throat. Why must he always look so devastatingly handsome? He was dressed in white shorts, sneakers and a black V-necked cashmere sweater. It was the first time she had ever seen him so casually dressed and it seemed to add a touch of boyishness to his manliness which she found extremely appealing. His eyes swept over her and she felt goosebumps rise.

'Those shorts are fine,' he growled. 'And so is that T-shirt. But you'll need a sweater.'

Her heart raced across her chest. 'What for?'

'In case a breeze comes up.'

Her eyes widened. 'Am I to go too?'

His eyes held hers and she saw the devil dancing in them. 'You most certainly are.'

'But ... but Jessie didn't say anything about ...'

'I didn't tell Jessie. You wouldn't have considered it a personal invitation. Now get that sweater.'

She didn't need any further urging. A sweater was found and he helped her into the Rover to take her place next to him. Jessie immediately wrapped her little arms around Catherine's neck.

'Oh, Mummy!' she squealed. 'I'm so glad you're coming too. Now you won't be cross with me for going without you!'

Catherine's cheeks flooded with embarrassment as she felt Mike's inquisitive eyes on her face. They burned even more when she heard him drawl softly, 'You didn't really think we would go without you?'

'I . . . I . . .' She flashed him a look. He was looking rather pleased with himself. 'Well, yes, I did think that.'

'But you were wrong.' The devil was there, dancing again and she responded with a smile.

'Yes, I was wrong.' She sighed happily. There was certainly satisfaction in being wrong now and then. Mike was in a buoyant mood, the children were chatting happily in the back, and she—well, she was content just being with him, watching his tanned, strong hands on the wheel of the Rover, expertly guiding it along the road, his muscular thigh so close to her own, and every now and then the brush of his broad shoulder as he changed gears.

It was a relatively short drive to Mon Repos, where the largest concentration of nesting marine turtles gathered each year, making it the most accessible turtle rookery in the South Pacific Ocean region. When Mike turned off the main highway and on to a much narrower road leading up to the beach, Catherine commented on the broken line of shining, low black rock fences which enabled cattle to roam freely, much to the children's delight.

'The rock walls were built by the Melanesians,' Mike explained. 'They were brought over during the 1870's to work in the canefields. The Kanakas, as they were called, cleared the land of the volcanic rock and the rock was used to build fences. Most of the fences were eventually torn down and the rocks crushed and used in road building. There are still enough of them around though to remind us of how hard the Kanakas worked and how skilled they were. In fact,' he continued, 'the swimming basin at the northern end of our beach was built by them to give the early settlers a safe place to swim.' He added wryly, 'Not a bad effort when you consider they worked for twenty-five pounds a year, plus two sets of clothing and board and lodging.'

'But why do they call this place Mon Repos?' one of the children wanted to know. 'Isn't Mon Repos a French name?'

'It is indeed,' Mike answered, 'but it wasn't named by a Frenchman. It means "My Rest" or "My Retreat" and that's what a fellow by the name of Augustus Barton called his cane farm and sugar mill. It was his Kanaka workers who built that rock wall.'

The sky was streaked with glorious shades of pinks, reds and golds as they pulled into the car park of the turtle rookery. When the flamboyantly beautiful colours disappeared, dusk would settle in. Mike switched off the ignition and turned sideways in his seat to directly address the children.

'One of the greatest aviators the world has ever known was hardly more than a boy when he made his first solo flight off this very beach. He reached a grand height of thirty feet, which was considered quite an accomplishment at the time. His name was Bert Hinkler and when he went to live in England he named his home Mon Repos. That same house was dismantled and brought back to Bundaberg, his birthplace, re-erected and renamed Hinkler House as a memorial to the city's famous son.' He added seriously, almost solemnly, 'Think about him and what he achieved when you're walking on the beach.'

Mike's guests had already arrived at the car park and were waiting for them. Mike introduced Catherine and she was made to feel welcome. Renata was not among them and Catherine later learned that those

without children had elected to stay back at the
mansion. Mike took charge of the group and explained how the turtles were easily disturbed by lights,
noise and movement, especially when leaving the surf,
crossing the beach and digging their nesting chambers.

'Don't make any sudden noises,' he warned, 'and
don't shine your torches on her or touch her until she
begins laying her eggs.' He handed each a small torch.
'These are under three volts. The turtles won't be affected by them but, even so, keep their use to a
minimum.'

Tickets were required and their numbers called
before small groups were allowed on the beach.
Catherine and Mike along with Jessie and Lucy made
their own small group. It was now totally dark, the
only light coming from the stars in the sky. Catherine
took hold of Jessie's hand and Mike held Lucy's. The
two little girls linked their free hands and they became
a foursome. They made their way slowly across the
sand, speaking only in hushed whispers. Mike suddenly stopped, bringing the others to a halt.

'Look!' He pointed to a huge lumbering object
desperately trying to break free of the pounding surf.

'It's a turtle!' Jessie and Lucy exclaimed excitedly.
Mike led them to a sheltered spot by the bottom of a
sand dune where they sat down to watch.

The great female loggerhead had managed to break
free of the surf. She moved laboriously across the
drifting sand, every inch an exhausting effort, for she
was not designed for land travel. Finally she came to
rest almost by their feet. They hardly dared breathe
as the great turtle began to construct a nesting
chamber, using her legs and feet like flippers to sweep
away a deep, wide hole in preparation for her eggs.

When the chamber was completed to her satisfaction, the mammoth creature began laying her eggs. Mike motioned them to switch on their small torches and, as he had predicted, the turtle was far too occupied with the business of depositing glistening snow-white eggs into the nesting chamber to be disturbed by them. The children gently patted her head and, when Catherine did the same, she noticed huge tears streaming from the great turtle's eyes. A lump of sympathy rose in Catherine's throat. 'She's *crying*!' she whispered.

Mike smiled into the darkness and put his arm around her slender shoulders and drew her close to his side. 'They're not real tears,' he murmured softly against her ear. 'It's only salt water.'

With her dozens of eggs laid, the turtle covered them with sand and, without resting, turned and began the arduous journey back to the charging foam-capped surf. The small group remained silent for several moments after she had disappeared into the mysterious depths, feeling subdued and awed by the experience they had just witnessed. Finally they rose to their feet and, as quietly as they had come, returned to the car park. Some of their party had already returned and others soon joined them. Everyone was strangely silent, still humbled by nature at its finest. The children Mike had transported returned with their own parents and Lucy was invited to spend the night with Jessie.

When they arrived back at Dune Cottage, Catherine remembered the chicken stew. She turned to Mike.

'Have you had dinner?'

She saw his teeth gleam white as he smiled into the dark interior of the Rover. 'Am I about to receive a personal invitation?'

Catherine flushed. 'It's not much. Only chicken stew.'

'Sounds great!'

And it was. The girls set the table, Mike opened a bottle of white wine, and Catherine reheated the stew and popped a crusty loaf into the oven. Mike was cheerful, the two little girls openly adoring him, and Catherine could tell they were thrilled that the four of them should be dining together. The kitchen was small, with Mike the centre of attention, his sheer size and height dominating every square inch, his voice reaching out and filling the corners, filling her heart, bringing life and vitality to their little group, his gentle teasing of the little girls making them laugh. Catherine laughed too, the rich, warm sounds adding even more warmth to the room, and her eyes sparkled and her love grew.

They sat at the kitchen table, with the soft glow of the overhead lamp shining down on them, their voices soft now against the sound of the waves drifting on to the beach and the rustle of the palms against the eaves. Several times Catherine met Mike's eyes, and she flushed at what she saw in them and knew he was in no hurry to leave. Not once had he mentioned their earlier row, and for this she was grateful. It would have spoiled a perfect evening.

The girls insisted on helping with the dishes and Catherine knew this was because they too wanted the evening to go on forever, or for as long as the adults would allow. When the dishes had been washed, dried and put away, she steered them into the bathroom and

poured water into the old-fashioned tub. While
Catherine fetched towels and nighties, she could hear
Mike still in the kitchen and, from the sounds he was
making, knew he was making them coffee.
Wonderful! She left the girls to their bath and joined
him on the veranda.

Mike had placed two steaming mugs of coffee on
the cane table centred between the two matching cane
chairs. But he wasn't sitting down. His broad back
was facing her as he stood looking out to sea, his
hands on the veranda rail, the soft breeze teasing his
hair. For a moment Catherine simply stood there,
framed in the doorway, her heart melting at the sight
of him. His white shorts seemed to glow against the
darkness of his skin and the black of his cashmere
sweater. His hair had grown a little longer since she
had first met him and she loved the way it seemed to
curl against the nape of his neck and almost touch
the edge of the sweater. Her hands trembled and her
fingertips tingled, for she longed to touch that hair,
feel its wiry texture, coil it around her fingers, feel
the shape of that proud, aristocratic head beneath her
palms.

He must have known she was there, for he turned
slightly, capturing her with his eyes and her heartbeats quickened for his eyes were dark and mysterious, curiously molten, and she was hypnotised by
them.

He didn't ask her to join him. There wasn't a need.
His eyes beckoned to her and she obeyed, crossing
over to him like being drawn by an invisible thread.
His eyes glowed brilliant in the darkness, intent upon
her face. He reached up and touched her cheek and
smiled when she shivered. His finger traced the

smooth curve and followed the line of her jaw down
to the slender column of her neck. He turned fully,
his back now against the rail, leaning against it, and
he pulled her to stand between his legs. She felt immediately that he was fully aroused and an answering
heat surged through her.

'A woman has the advantage over a man,' he said
huskily, 'for she can hide what he cannot!'

'I don't think I can hide ... anything from you,'
Catherine whispered and her voice sounded thick and
strange to her ears. His hands burned on the small of
her back and she gasped when they slipped lower, his
fingers curling around her hips, but he made no move
to draw her closer. Catherine placed her hands on his
chest, her palms flattened against hard muscle and
bone. She moved them slowly upwards, until her arms
entwined his neck, her fingers splaying through the
thick wiry texture of his hair. Their eyes were locked,
hazel to blue, their depths darkening, their mouths
barely a whisper apart. Suddenly, she was pressed
against him and a small cry tore from her throat as
his mouth closed over hers, his hard lips burning with
a passion that sent her fragile senses reeling. Her arms
tightened around him, her body urgent with need as
she moved closer against him. She heard him groan,
deep within his throat, and she cried out his name, a
pleading murmur against his mouth. His fingers
tugged at the hem of her shorts, moving beneath the
lace of her panties, but the barrier was too much, the
fabric of her shorts preventing entry. With a strangled
moan, his hands moved down her thighs, up and over
her hips and Catherine felt her T-shirt being pulled
free and his hands on her fevered skin, burning a trail
up to her naked breasts. His tongue moved against

the warm, moist intimacy of her mouth, drinking in her sweetness, tasting her urgent desire, muffling the small pleading cries gurgling from her throat. His huge hands closed over her breasts, his thumbs stroking the erected nubs, and she arched against him, her nails digging into his scalp. He drew her still closer against him, their clothing a cruel barrier against their need. It was only when she felt him pull impatiently at her T-shirt did a small measure of sanity return and with it the realisation they weren't alone.

'No!' she cried, her gasping voice filled with a frenzied panic.

Mike drew back, the molten black of his eyes gazing down at her as she struggled to restore her clothing. Her hands flew to her hair in a frenzied attempt to tidy it and he frowned as he dragged long fingers through his own thick scrub. His hands reached out and grabbed her again, pulling her against his hard arousal, his lips burning at her throat, his teeth nibbling on the smooth, creamy texture of her silky skin.

'I can't keep this up,' he ground against her neck. 'It's madness tempting each other this way.'

'I know,' she whispered, her eyes dazed, her body straining convulsively against his. She was consumed with a burning, aching pain and the sudden rush of tears which swept to her eyes told him her suffering, her need, was as great as his own.

'Move into the house.' His voice was urgent. 'We can have privacy, put an end to these ridiculous games, give each other what we both want.' His hands gripped her shoulders, his fingers digging almost cruelly into her soft flesh. 'Say yes, Catherine!' he demanded hoarsely, a fierce light gleaming in his eyes.

It would be so easy for her to do as he asked. And they *would* have privacy. Privacy to make love, to give into the tormentingly sweet desires which rocked their bodies, enflamed their senses. It would be foolish and dishonest to deny she wanted him as much as he wanted her. But she *loved* him! Her desires weren't only physical; her feelings ran much deeper than that. She loved everything about him. His smile could send her pulses racing just as quickly as his kiss. His hands and arms could weave their magic on her tender skin, send her nerve-ends tingling, but, even more importantly, they warmed her and made her feel . . . safe, protected and wonderfully secure. Her love for him was special, precious, unique. To her, it would become soiled somehow, tarnished, if she had to betray her tender love by sneaking into his room in the dead of night, or have him come to her, when all were asleep in his household. She couldn't do this to herself . . . nor could she betray her daughter's trust and her mother's.

Mike watched her struggle, saw the emotions move across her delicate face. His eyes deepened and darkened and when she opened her mouth to speak he sighed deeply, shook his head ever so slightly and pressed his finger against her trembling lips.

'It's all right,' he said gruffly. 'I know what you're going to say and you're absolutely right.' There was regret in his voice as he added softly, 'It's far too late to simply become a house guest.'

'Yes,' she whispered, and while she was grateful for his understanding her heart yearned for him to say something more, something to give her hope, to make her feel his feelings ran deeper than the mere physical. But no such words were forthcoming. She lowered her eyes to hide her disappointment, mask her hurt, but the pain in her heart refused to go away and she raised her hand to her chest in a futile effort to soothe her torment, ease her anguish.

Mike's hand slipped down to her wrist and he could feel the rapid beat of her pulse. He reached for her other hand, pried it away from her aching heart. Her eyes moved slowly up to his and what she saw filled her with a new agony. There was no passion left in those dark, mysterious orbs. The heat, the desire, had been replaced with a cold sombreness, but even more distressing was the haunting ache of loneliness she saw hidden there, a deep-rooted sadness which instinct told her she was never meant to see. And this new knowledge made her earlier hurt seem like a mere scratch compared to what she was feeling now.

'Our coffee will be getting cold,' he told her, his voice low, guarded, a rumble against the wind and the restless pounding of the sea.

'Yes,' she nodded, her own voice a mere whisper above the aching thrashing of her heart. Her fingers entwined around his and he tightened his hold in a bruising grip before releasing her hand altogether. He walked briskly across the veranda, his straight back and broad shoulders making her wonder if she really had seen what she knew she had in his eyes. He was in total control, master of himself and all that he ruled, and it was there for anyone to see. But Catherine knew, as she walked slowly over to join him, that she had seen far more. She had glimpsed into his very soul.

Mike picked up their coffees, placed them on the floor, moved the small cane table out of the way, shoved the two chairs together, picked up the mugs, motioned for Catherine to sit and, when she had settled herself, handed her the mug. She raised it unsteadily to her lips while he sat down beside her, their shoulders brushing as he stretched out his long, tanned and muscular legs in front of him, ankles crossed casually. Their coffee was cold but neither commented on this fact, nor did they seem to even notice. For a while they didn't speak, their eyes fixed on the silvery caps of the incoming tide. The lounge behind them was in darkness, the only lights coming from the soft luminous glow of the Christmas tree sparkling through the opened window facing the veranda.

Catherine leaned back in her chair and gazed up at the velvet blackness of the sky, studded with twinkling pearl drops. 'When you build your resort,' she began softly, 'your guests will never tire of that sky. Especially if they come from any big city. You can barely see any stars when you live in a city.' She laughed a small, shaky little laugh. 'The first time Jessie and I saw the moon rise we...we were frightened. We were sitting here, in the dark, and suddenly this enormous fiery red ball seemed to rise straight out of the sea! It was majestic and beautiful and scary all at the same time.' She gave him a sideways glance to see if he thought this was ridiculous but there was no mockery in the midnight blue of his eyes.

'It is a phenomenal sight,' he quietly agreed.

'And they will love the peace and quiet,' Catherine continued, her eyes fully on his face now, wanting to draw him into a discussion about his resort, wanting desperately to erase the dark brooding in his eyes. 'Will you have one big building, like a...a hotel, or several smaller ones like a motel?'

He looked her straight in the eyes and she flushed slightly, because that look told her he knew what she was trying to do. A softness entered his eyes and gentled the hard line of his mouth. But there was no excitement in his voice when he spoke, only a flat account of his plans.

'There will be cottages, not unlike this one, and each dwelling will have its own tropical garden, with its own exotic birds and native wildlife and, most importantly, total privacy.'

'Sounds wonderful!' Catherine breathed, and her eyes lit up as she imagined it. 'And they will have their own private cove to swim in.'

His eyes swept the expansive view of the moonlit cove flanked by the majestic dunes. Why did they always remind him of gigantic sandcastles? he wondered impatiently.

'Part of the cove will be set aside for swimming,' he told her and she heard the almost stiff reluctance in his voice as he continued, 'It's a natural harbour, deep and just the right size. Guests can bring their own yachts if they have them, and for those who don't I'll provide them. Either way, each cottage will have its own mooring.'

'A marina!' She tried to picture the peaceful cove and what it would look like with a dozen or more yachts bobbing above the gentle waves. She decided she liked the picture. 'Sounds wonderful,' she said again.

He leaned towards her and suddenly his voice was filled with enthusiasm, the confidence and excitement of a creator with a new masterpiece to unfold.

'Think of it, Catherine! Think of a resort that not only offers total privacy but a chance to sail through the Whitsundays, explore the Great Barrier Reef, cruise over to Fraser Island and walk on the largest sand island in the world. They can sit on their own decks, watch the humpback whales frolic beside them, the dolphins playing around them.'

His hand was on her arm, warm and firm against her bare skin, sending her pulses skydiving once more as she listened, totally enraptured as he told her of his plans. If Mike Donahue wanted to build the finest, most exciting, most impressive resort the world had ever seen and build it right here, where Dune Cottage now stood, where her petunias were now growing in a wild profusion of glorious colours, and where her mother and Albert had come to escape the confines of the mansion walls, then . . . so be it. She was with him all the way!

'Sounds wonderful!' she murmured for the third time, and lost herself in the eyes which were as dark and as gripping as the man himself. The tingling sensation in the pit of her stomach intensified, made her want to move closer to him, to feel his hard body against the sizzling currents of her own. His eyes gleamed in the moonlight and he reached for her hand, sending shivers spiralling down her spine as his long, dark fingers entwined around hers. He lifted her hand and, with his eyes locked to hers in a visual embrace, kissed the tip of each of her pink-tipped fingers.

'What was your life like in Brisbane?' he asked her softly, startling her with the abruptness of such a question and forcing her to swiftly gather her moonstruck wits and concentrate on an answer.

'It . . . it was pretty ordinary, I guess. Nothing . . . nothing special, not very interesting.'

If she had hoped to satisfy his curiosity with such blatant evasiveness, she was sadly mistaken.

'Where did you live? What did you do? I know you studied but what else did you do?' His eyes were darkly compelling, intent upon her face.

'Well, in the beginning I worked at a lot of jobs which offered long hours, little pay and no chance of advancement. I put Jessie into child-minding centres.' Pain entered her eyes as she remembered those long, hard years. 'In the evenings I taught myself to type on an old typewriter I bought, hoping to increase my chances of getting better jobs with better hours. But...' She shrugged her small shoulders. 'Technology was way ahead of me. Typing was fine but I didn't have any computer skills. But it made me realise a better education was what I needed. I dragged out my old school records and my marks were high enough to give me entrance into university. Fortunately I was able to arrange my timetable to fit in with my part-time jobs.'

'And now you're a teacher.' His smile was warm upon her face as he said the words and she saw pride in his eyes... as though he was *proud* of her accomplishments. A moonbeam pierced her heart and glowed in her eyes. 'Where did you live?' he asked, and she knew he wanted to know everything.

'In an apartment near the university which was also close to a child-minding centre and my jobs.' She thought of the dark, dingy rooms which had been their home for too many years and a cloud passed over her eyes. 'It's so wonderful being here at Dune Cottage,' she continued softly. 'Jessie and I lived on the third floor. Our only view was that of other apartment blocks and when we opened our door it was only to see a dark corridor with a line of closed doors. Here, we step right outside into the sunshine and every window has a view of the ocean and the beach and the dunes.' She added simply, sincerely, 'I guess that's why we love it so much.'

She felt a sudden tension in his hands as he still held hers and something slipped fiercely into his eyes.

'What about your social life?' he asked gruffly. 'Was there . . . ?' He cleared his throat and she smiled because she knew what he was wanting to know and was too proud and possibly too arrogant to ask.

'All my spare time was spent with Jessie. It hurt to leave her for so many hours every day and . . . and I never once met a man whose company I preferred over hers.'

Her answer seemed to please him. A flash of triumph burned briefly in the glittering depths of his eyes before he took in a deep, satisfying breath and exhaled it just as deeply. He released her hand and his arm went around her shoulders as he drew her close to him and she felt his hard warm cheek against her own. The small dingy apartment in Brisbane, the lonely struggle for survival miraculously disappeared and she was left with only the magic of him.

The girls came on to the veranda to say goodnight, smelling sweetly of toothpaste and soap. Catherine instinctively tried to move from the enclosure of Mike's arm but he held her firmly in place.

'Goodnight, Mummy,' Jessie said, and kissed Catherine's cheek.

'Goodnight, Daddy,' Lucy said, and kissed Mike's cheek. Holding hands, they skipped back into the cottage and within seconds their heads popped through the opened window.

'Goodnight, Mummy and Daddy!' they sang out in mischievous unison before ducking their heads back in again and running into Jessie's bedroom amid a fit of the giggles.

There was a stunned silence on the veranda. Catherine held her breath while staring straight in front of her. She felt Mike's arm stiffen around her shoulders. He was the one who broke the pregnant silence.

'What did they say?' His voice sounded choked.

Catherine's lips moved silently as she struggled for the words. 'They said . . . goodnight, Mummy and Daddy.'

'That's what I thought they said!' He added with a scowl, 'Scamps!'

Catherine nodded. 'Imps!' she agreed.

And under cover of the blackness of the hot still night, she smiled a secret smile.

Mike rose abruptly from his chair. He looked at her upturned face, the moon reflected in her lovely eyes.

'I think. . . .'

'Yes?' she asked breathlessly.

'I think you and Jessie had better come over to my place for Christmas dinner. Would twelve o'clock suit?'

'Twelve would be just fine,' Catherine agreed, and bells chimed in her heart.

CHAPTER TEN

BUNDABERG had a famous son in Bert Hinkler. It also had a famous daughter. Gladys Moncrieff was born in the pleasant coastal town in 1892, the same year as Hinkler, and went on to become one of the world's greatest operatic stars. As Catherine and Wade entered the Moncrieff Theatre, named in honour of the star, a soft breeze caught the hem of her white chiffon dress and swirled it around her long, slender legs. As she hastened to hold it down, her eyes caught Mike across the crowded foyer.

Her heart gave an involuntary thump before it danced across her chest. He looked spectacular in a black dinner-jacket and crisp white shirt, and with his impressive height and dark colouring was the centre of attention of many an admiring female eye. Clinging possessively to his arm was the beautiful Renata, her long blonde hair magnificent against the black velvet of her dress. Mike gave Catherine a brief nod, merely acknowledging her presence, cast a narrowed look at Wade and turned his attention back to his friends. Catherine's heart sank miserably to the pit of her stomach.

'Would you like a glass of wine?' Wade asked.

'That would be nice,' Catherine murmured, and watched as he made his way to the crowded bar. Mike and his group were stationed near it and she tried desperately to keep from looking at them but her eyes refused to obey. Every time Mike smiled or laughed or listened attentively to something being said, her eyes were on him. Whenever he paid Renata the least bit of attention, her nails dug into the palms of her hands. She knew she was jealous, a sickening feeling but she simply couldn't help herself. And as much as it hurt to see her love with someone else, she knew it would be worse not to see him at all.

Gwen, one of the ladies she had been introduced to at Mon Repos and whose son they had driven in the Rover, spotted Catherine and broke away from the group. Catherine had especially liked the young brown-eyed brunette. She had a warm, unaffected personality and her husband Jake was a great friend of Mike's, an engineer who worked closely with him on his building projects.

'I didn't see you arrive,' Gwen said, an easy smile spreading across her expressive face. 'I thought you were coming with us but Mike said you had made other arrangements.'

Catherine glanced across at Wade waiting in line at the bar. Gwen followed her look. 'Is he someone special?'

'No, just a friend.'

'You turned down an invitation from Mike to go out with a friend?' Gwen asked with a surprised chuckle. 'I like that, but I'll bet Mike didn't.'

'He didn't ... at first.' Her eyes swept over at Mike in time to see him place his arm around Renata's shoulders as they studied the programme together. 'But ... he's got Renata.'

Again Gwen chuckled. 'He might have Renata but Renata doesn't have him.' She became serious. 'After the hell Mike's ex put him through, most of us feel it will be a long time before...' Gwen checked herself.

'Oops, sorry.' She held up her half-empty glass of champagne. 'This stuff makes me talk.'

But Catherine was desperate to hear more. 'Was Mike's ex-wife a model like Renata?' she probed.

'No, but she could have been. She's certainly beautiful enough. I haven't seen her in years but I doubt she's changed.' She added almost bitterly. 'A leopard can't change its spots. I'll bet she's giving her new husband a run for his money just as she did Mike.'

'You mean...she married Mike just for his money?'

Gwen nodded. 'And for the prestige and power it brings. What she didn't count on was the fact that Mike expected her to be a true partner in every sense of the word. You see, Mike has made us a team. His projects take us around the world. Where the men go, the wives and children follow. Some of the countries and places offer very little in home comforts. Gail could never adjust. In fact, she refused to adjust. She simply stayed home and amused herself with his money. When she knew he'd had enough she managed to get herself pregnant. After Lucy was born she was heard to boast that the child was her ticket to the Donahue fortune!'

Catherine was horrified. 'How shocking!'

Gwen nodded. 'Gail knew Mike was besotted by his little daughter. Lucy takes after his mother, with her colouring, and he was very fond of her. Gail continued to live like royalty, going on world cruises while Mike was away and leaving the child in the care of nannies. In fact, she met her present husband on one of the cruises and finally gave Mike his divorce. We figured he must have had more money than Mike. He's also old enough to be her *grandfather*!' She placed a hand on Catherine's arm. 'Jake just gave me a signal. I think we're going to find our seats now.' She hesitated and then smiled warmly at Catherine. 'Don't give up on Mike,' she said softly. 'I know you love him. I saw it in your eyes at Mon Repos and it's there when you speak about him. I think he has feelings about you, too, but he probably hasn't realised it yet.' She sighed deeply. 'Men can be so stupid about such things!'

Gwen hurried off to join her husband and Catherine watched as they made their way to the stairs. Mike and Renata were ahead of them and Catherine's eyes remained glued to his broad back until he disappeared from her view. He hadn't spoken to her, not a single word, and, despite Gwen's words of encouragement, disappointment burned in her eyes.

Wade came up to her. He didn't have the wine. 'Sorry,' he apologised, looking sheepish. 'By the time I got through the crowd, it was time to close the bar.' A warning signal was heard. 'The show's about to start.' He took her arm. 'We'll get something at interval.'

Wade presented their tickets to the usher and they were escorted to their seats. As soon as they sat down, Catherine scanned the crowd for Mike. She saw him almost immediately. She would know that proud, aristocratic head anywhere. When the curtain went up, Catherine settled in her seat to watch him and to think about what Gwen had told her.

Every word was played over and over in her mind, from the unhappy life Mike had shared with his ex-wife to the fact that Gwen had guessed she was in love with the man. But the words she cherished most and played the most often were the ones, 'I think he has feelings about you too but he probably hasn't realised it yet!'

Could it be true? she wondered joyously as she lovingly watched him. There was no denying the powerful physical attraction they had for each other. Hers had grown into love and had started with the stories told about him. Had his feelings deepened as well?

She loved everything about him. The way his eyes crinkled at the corners when he smiled, the deep cleft in his chin, his eyes so brilliantly blue and his mouth... She sighed restlessly.

Wade glanced at her. 'Is everything all right?'

'Yes, why?'

'You keep making funny sounds.'

'What sorts of sounds?' Her face turned scarlet. 'Never mind. I'm sure it wasn't me!'

Catherine forced herself to concentrate on the performance but it wasn't easy. Each time Mike so much as moved in his chair, her eyes returned to him. Whenever his dark head tilted towards Renata's, a spear of red-hot jealousy pierced her heart. When the audience burst into spontaneous laughter she heard only his laugh. And once, when she wasn't looking at him, he turned and looked at her, finding her just as easily as she had found him among the sea of faces in the darkened theatre. Her eyes moved instantly to join with his and it was as if they silently caressed each other, there in the dark, rows and rows apart!

When the interval lights came on, Catherine watched anxiously to see if Mike would remain in his seat or go downstairs to the lobby. Whatever he did, she would do.

'Would you like to go down for some refreshments?' Wade enquired, and added with a grin, 'I'm sure to get through to the bar this time.'

After a brief discussion, Mike and a few from his party rose from their chairs. Catherine rose from hers.

'Yes, I think I would.' She smiled. 'But instead of wine, maybe a glass of orange juice.'

The theatre crowd scrambled for the stairs. Catherine was soon separated from Wade. Halfway down the stairs she was pushed from behind. She experienced several seconds of fear as she started to fall. A strong arm reached out for her and caught her. She drew in his fresh, clean scent, looked into the deep blue of his eyes and felt the warmth of his hard, lean body as he drew her protectively to his side.

And she was reminded of the time she had stumbled on the stairs leading up to his study. He had steadied her and held on to her hand and she had been so nervous, not wanting to be alone with him because he had affected her even then. He smiled down at her and his eyes crinkled at the corners and his teeth gleamed white against the darkness of his lips. His arm tightened around her waist.

'Don't be in such a hurry,' he growled softly, and she flushed because she realised she had practically been racing down the stairs. She wondered what he would say if she told him she had been running to meet him, to catch even a glimpse of him, maybe even find herself standing next to him. After all, anything could happen in a crowded foyer of a theatre.

Mike steered her safely down the remaining stairs and guided her across the lobby. 'Where's your friend?' he enquired coldly.

Catherine blinked. 'Friend?'

'Your date.'

'You mean Wade?'

Anger flickered in his eyes. 'That's what you called him before.'

'I ... I don't know.' She glanced around. 'I ... I thought he was right behind me.'

'You weren't running away from him, were you?'

'Running away ... ? Why, no ... no, of course not. Oh, there he is ... at the bar. He ... he couldn't get through last time. He's getting me a drink ... a glass of orange juice.' She knew she was babbling, sounding suspiciously of an awkward schoolgirl but she simply couldn't help herself. Mike had steered her into a corner of the lobby where potted palms sheltered them from the rest of the crowd. It was strangely intimate, deliciously private. His arm was still around her waist and he held on to her, lifting her chin with his free hand, his eyes devouring the exquisite beauty of her face.

'You look lovely tonight, Catherine,' he murmured and touched her mouth with his in a brief searing kiss before tracing the outline of her delicate cheek.

'Say goodnight to Curtis after the show and drive back with me,' he urged. 'We're having a small party, a bit of dancing ...' He kissed her again and she felt his mounting passion. 'Say *yes!*' His hand rose and stopped just beneath the swell of her breast. A shiver of desire swept through her and she was grateful for the privacy the screen of palms gave them. He turned her slightly so the length of her body was pressed against his. His hands burned on her bare shoulders before sweeping down her arms. He stiffened suddenly as his hand closed around her wrist. He lifted her arm and removed his hand. Her gold watch gleamed up at them.

'I'd almost forgotten about this,' he stated stiffly, his voice sounding suddenly hard and cold. He tore his eyes from the watch and settled them on her face. She was bewildered and not just a little frightened by the liquid fire blazing in their depths. '*Almost!*' he added in a snarl. He took a deep breath and let it out slowly. Disappointment replaced the fury in his eyes and for some strange reason Catherine felt far more affected by it. 'I wondered at the time who was the recipient of such an expensive gift,' he ground out. 'Now I know!'

A picture flashed through Catherine's mind. A picture of Mike holding the accounts in his study, stopping at one, before continuing. The picture was followed by another, only this time it was of her mother doing the very same thing. They had been looking at the account for her watch... her very *expensive* watch!

'Your father gave it to me for a graduation gift,' she explained. 'I... I realise it must have cost a small fortune and... and that's why I haven't worn it, why you haven't seen it. I thought the salt air might damage it, so... so I... so I kept it for a special occasion.'

She realised immediately she had somehow managed to say the wrong thing. Fury once again flared in his eyes.

'A special occasion!' he repeated with a seething contempt. 'You consider a date with that... that idiot... a *special occasion*?'

'Well, no, that's not what I meant!'

His hands gripped her shoulders and she winced. 'What *did* you mean?' he snarled.

'I meant ... the theatre ... getting dressed up.'

His eyes moved like blazing torches down the soft filmy chiffon of her dress and returned once more to her troubled face.

'I wasn't hiding it from you, if that's what you're thinking!' she suddenly blurted, tears forming in her eyes. 'I didn't want to offend your father by refusing to accept it but if you think I should, I'll willingly give it back to him.' Her eyes were blurred as she looked down at the watch. 'It's ... it's not practical anyway.' She started to take it off but he stopped her.

'Don't be ridiculous. The watch is yours. It's far too late to be giving it back.'

Catherine shook her head. She couldn't keep it. Not now. Her fingers trembled on the clasp as she clumsily tried to undo it. A tear rolled down her cheek and splashed on to the crystal. She heard a sharp sigh.

'Damn, Catherine, don't you ever listen?' His hand, so huge and brown against the small paleness of her own, expertly redid the clasp. She looked up at him and through her tears saw his face was contorted with an emotion she couldn't understand. A sharp pain stabbed her heart and something vital within her seemed to wither and die. She looked achingly up at him. She loved him but she knew now he could never love her. And the reason was simple. He didn't trust her. And after hearing Gwen's account of the voraciousness of his ex-wife, it was easy to understand that he thought most women were tarred from the same brush.

It was a relief when Wade found them. He looked uncertainly from Catherine's pain-filled face to

Mike's, which was as grim and as unrelenting as a master torturer.

'I ... I've got your juice,' Wade said awkwardly to Catherine.

'Th-thank you.' She felt Mike stiffen and his hands balled into huge fists as he glared at the younger man. For a terrifying second Catherine actually thought he might hit him. Instead he turned sharply on his heel and disappeared around the potted palms.

The last half of the performance was a nightmare for Catherine, and when the final curtain came down she gave a sigh of relief. The drive back to the beach seemed to take forever. The kitchen light was on in the little cottage but, other than that, there was total darkness. When she opened the door and stepped inside, her eyes fell on a note propped against the fruit bowl in the centre of the table. Catherine snatched it up. It was from her mother.

Darling,
Jessie was complaining of a sore throat and upset tummy so I've taken her over to the house to give her something for both. Don't worry, I'm sure it's nothing serious. Hope you had a great time. See you in the morning. Mother

Catherine studied the note. Jessie had been in the pink of health when she had left only a few hours ago. But experience had taught her that children could become seriously ill in a short space of time. The mansion was filled with the children of Mike's guests and with Christmas so close Catherine didn't want Jessie infecting them. She was surprised that her mother hadn't thought of that, but then supposed she had the child with her in her own private quarters well away from the main body of the house.

But still, if Jessie was ill, and even though her mother was convinced it was nothing serious, she should be in her own little bed, with her own mother taking care of her. And…she didn't want to give Mike any further reason to accuse her unjustly. Catherine jumped into her MG and roared towards the mansion. There seemed to be cars parked everywhere and from the back came the sounds of a party already in progress. With any luck at all she could enter undetected, make her way up to her mother's rooms, grab Jessie and return to the cottage…and finally deal with her crumbling heart.

And it was all so easy. The evening was hot and the French doors were opened on to the veranda to take full advantage of any cooling breezes from the ocean. She slipped through one of the doors and raced up the sweeping staircase, down the long wide corridor and finally to her mother's quarters, which were connected to Albert's. Catherine tapped lightly on the door and entered when Betty answered.

Betty and Albert, dressed in pyjamas and light dressing-gowns, were seated in plush armchairs, watching television and sipping on mugs of hot chocolate. Astonished, Catherine could only stare at them. It had never occurred to her that they had actually grown so intimate, even though she had realised they were companionable. They looked so cosy, so comfortable, so *right* together that it took a few seconds for Catherine to realise she had been contemplating asking her mother to give up her job and move into a flat with herself and Jessie in Bundaberg. That idea had been born that evening during the second half of the performance when she had felt she could no longer be in such close contact to Mike. And somehow she had felt she must rescue her mother from him as well.

'Catherine!' Betty exclaimed, surprised but obviously pleased to see her daughter. 'Surely you haven't come over to enquire about Jessie? I told you it was nothing serious.'

'I know but I would feel better if she was with me and I don't want her infecting the other children.'

Betty and Albert exchanged amused glances. 'It turned out to be a false alarm,' Albert chuckled. 'She only wanted to be with our Lucy.'

A feeling of helplessness washed over Catherine. Didn't anyone want to be with her any more? Her own child broke every rule in the book, invented impossible excuses, even feigned sickness to get over to the mansion to be with Lucy. Her own mother, a trained nurse, had allowed herself to be hoodwinked, no doubt deliberately, so she could return and be with Albert. A wave of self-pity swept aside the feeling of helplessness and she savoured it for just a few seconds before pushing it firmly aside. She knew her feelings of despair had been prompted by Mike's reaction to her watch and the condemnation she had seen in his eyes.

'I see you're wearing your watch, Catherine,' Betty remarked as though reading her thoughts. 'Come closer, dear, and show it to us.'

Catherine went over to them and put out her arm. She held her breath, half expecting Albert to ask her where she got it. 'Gold looks beautiful against your skin, Catherine,' he said. 'I would have liked to have something engraved on the back but there wasn't time.' He smiled up at her. 'Not if you were to receive it in time for your graduation.'

Catherine looked down into his kindly blue eyes and caring face. She felt tears burn at the backs of her eyes. 'Thank you,' she whispered, and impulsively reached down and kissed his cheek.

At the door, she paused. 'I'll check in on the girls. If Jessie is still awake I'll take her back to the cottage. I don't want her thinking she can try this little caper again!' She smiled at them and let herself quietly out the door.

Lucy's bedroom was at the opposite wing of the house and Catherine hurried in that direction. Now that she had calmed down and feeling more her usual self she had a distinct sensation of unease about traipsing along the mansion's corridors on her own. The feeling was so acute, she glanced nervously over her shoulder several times, half expecting to see someone watching her. It was with no small measure of relief when she finally reached Lucy's bedroom door. She nodded knowingly when she heard the little girls laughing and chatting behind it. She knocked softly and stepped inside.

The girls were sitting on the bed, playing with oodles of costume jewellery. In fact, they were covered in it, from beads and necklaces draped around their necks, earrings dangling from their ears, bracelets strung around their wrists and rings decorating their fingers.

'Mummy!' Jessie exclaimed, guiltily, 'What are you doing here?'

'I'm here to take you back to the cottage, you little imposter.' She ruffled both their heads. 'Now where's your robe?' She found it on the floor beside the bed. 'Hurry along, Jessie, take off that…that…' Catherine

stared at the necklace around Jessie's neck. A gasp
rose to her throat. It was made of diamonds, *real* diamonds! Her stunned eyes took in the rest and she
realised she was staring at a wealth of diamond rings,
necklaces, gold chains, bracelets and clips worth a
fortune. Rubies, emeralds, diamonds, gold and silver
glittered from the children's necks, arms, wrists and
fingers. Catherine was speechless, horrified. When she
did manage to speak, she hardly recognised the sound
of her own voice.

'Where did you get this? Whose is it? My God, and
you've been *playing* with it!'

'It's all right, it's mine,' Lucy explained calmly.
'Grandma left it to me in her will.'

'But surely you're not allowed to *play* with it?'

'Well, no-o, not really. Not until I'm eighteen.'

'Why are you playing with it now?'

'I just wanted to show it to Jessie.'

Catherine turned to look at her daughter. 'Jessie,
take all of that off this *instant*! You too, Lucy.' Her
eyes fell on a large, beautifully carved ivory case. The
jewellery obviously belonged in it. While the girls were
removing the precious items and placing them in the
case under Catherine's watchful eyes, all she could
think about was that if one piece went missing,
somehow she would be blamed. It was a crazy thought
but so far it had been a crazy evening. When the box
was finally filled, she turned to Lucy. 'Now where
does this belong?'

'In Daddy's study. There's a safe behind one of the
pictures. The key to it is in Daddy's desk.'

Catherine felt her throat closing up. Of course it
would be in Mike's study! Where else? Catherine held

the case out to Lucy. 'Take it back!' she ordered shakily.

'I don't want to.'

'You *must*!'

'I'll do it in the morning.'

'You will do it *now*!'

Lucy started to whimper. 'Only if you and Jessie come with me.'

'All right,' Catherine agreed frantically. 'But we must be very quiet.'

Catherine's heart was in her throat the whole time it took to make their way to Mike's study. From the opened windows she could hear the party going on below and she silently prayed that he wouldn't suddenly decide to come upstairs. To her added horror, she saw the girls had left the safe door wide open, with the key still in the lock. The jewellery case was quickly installed, the safe locked and the key returned to a drawer in Mike's desk. Catherine whisked the girls back to Lucy's room to see the child safely in bed before making their own departure. Lucy kicked off her slippers and immediately gave a sharp cry of pain.

'Ouch!' she wailed. 'Something's cut my foot.'

Catherine quickly examined it. There was a small puncture wound and a few droplets of crimson blood. Lucy howled at the sight of it, convinced she would surely bleed to death. Catherine managed to quieten her down and got antiseptic and a roll of bandage from Lucy's adjoining bathroom.

'Look, Mummy,' Jessie said as Catherine bound Lucy's foot. 'This must be what Lucy stepped on.'

Catherine groaned aloud when she saw what Jessie was holding. A ruby ring, surrounded by glittering diamonds. It would have to be returned to the safe. Leaving Jessie behind to console the injured Lucy, Catherine once again made a lightning trip to Mike's study, the ring held securely in her hand. With the blood hammering in her ears and with that eerie sensation of being watched again, Catherine found the key in Mike's desk and quickly opened the safe. She pulled out the jewellery box and carefully lifted the top. The door to Mike's study burst open. Catherine whirled guiltily, her eyes rounded in fright. The box flew from her hands and the jewellery landed in soft thuds on to the carpeted floor.

Mike was framed in the doorway, Mrs Beasley behind him. They stared at her, Mrs Beasley's face cold, Mike's face black with anger. Nausea formed in the pit of Catherine's stomach and her frozen lips moved but no sound came through. She was mesmerised by Mike's eyes. They no longer seemed blue. They were black, and the devil's fires burned deep within them. Behind her, the opened safe gaped like a great black ominous hole!

CHAPTER ELEVEN

IT WAS a moment Catherine felt certain she would never forget. She stood frozen in front of the opened safe, imprisoned by the fierce lights blazing from the fiery depths of Mike's eyes.

'You may go, Mrs Beasley,' Mike ordered, his voice low, controlled, his eyes fixed on Catherine's pale face as he issued the command. Mrs Beasley backed out. Mike kicked the door shut with a well aimed blow from his heel.

He moved slowly towards her and stood directly in front of her. She could feel the hot, throbbing pulse of his anger and she took a cautionary step backwards. The opened safe door brushed against her hair and she gave a startled cry. Mike grabbed her wrist, his steel fingers biting into her fragile bones. He wrenched the ring from her hand.

'The watch wasn't enough!' he snarled. 'You wanted *more!*' His hands moved up to her shoulders and he shook her violently. Her hair flew about her face as though tossed by a raging wind. Still he shook her, her head snapping back and forth like a rag doll's, and when he finally released her she sank slowly to her knees, her head spinning and nausea rising to her throat. Through the tangled mass of her hair she could see his shoes, black and gleaming against the soft plushness of the carpet. Scattered around them were the priceless pieces of jewellery.

148

'Get up!' he snarled, and she struggled to obey his command but the room was whirling around her and she was terrified she was going to be sick. He reached down and pulled her to her feet and helped her into a chair. She pushed her hair back with shaking hands and looked at him. He was staring down at the pieces of jewellery on the floor. Slowly he bent and retrieved them, throwing them onto his desk. When he turned and looked at her she was shocked by the whiteness of his skin, the thin compressed line of his mouth. A ragged sigh tore from her throat. She knew she had already been judged and found guilty.

'What were you planning to do with it?' he asked bitterly. 'Pawn it?'

Her eyes were clouded with an unbearable hurt as she forced herself to meet his gaze. 'I was putting the ring back into the case,' she whispered and her eyes pleaded with him to believe her.

But instead of believing her, her answer only seemed to fuel his anger. His glittering glare left no room for mercy. His hands balled into fists and she shrank into her chair. 'Don't lie, Catherine,' he stated with an icy calm. 'Don't give me an excuse to break every bone in your body because, so help me God, that's exactly what I feel like doing!'

With superhuman effort, Catherine regained control of herself. She rose stiffly from her chair and faced him with a calmness she was far from feeling. Only the green flecks flashing in her eyes betrayed her true emotions. With her hair splashed wildly about her face and the high cut of her white chiffon dress circling her slender throat she appeared extremely young and oh, so vulnerable. Mike's eyes were fixed on that look.

'When I returned from the theatre I found a note from Mother telling me Jessie wasn't feeling well and that she had brought her over here. I was worried and came to check. I . . . I didn't want to disturb anyone and all the doors were opened so I let myself in.' Catherine hesitated. Was there any point in continuing? She tried to read his expression. Obviously he had decided to allow her to rattle off a story before passing sentence. Or was he thinking about calling in the authorities? His hand was by the telephone on his desk. Catherine took a deep breath and plunged on.

'Jessie wasn't sick after all. She was merely pretending so she could spend the night with Lucy. I went to Lucy's bedroom to get Jessie and I found them playing with the jewellery.'

Mike frowned and sat down on the edge of the desk. Catherine hurried on, the words now tumbling from her throat, eager to get this whole crazy mess over and done with. 'We took it back here and locked it in the safe but when we got back to Lucy's bedroom . . . found the ring on the floor and . . . and I brought it back and that's . . . that's when you . . . when you . . .' To Catherine's horror a great gulping sob tore from her throat. She covered her face with her hands while her shoulders shook. It had all been too much for her. All of it. Everything. Her sobs echoed around the silence of the room. A starched white handkerchief was thrust into her hands. But that was all. There were no words of comfort. No apologies. He had moved away from her to stand by the window, his broad back like a door, blocking her out. The ensuing silence was unbearable. Catherine pressed the handkerchief to her mouth and fled from the room.

Mike remained standing by the window for several minutes after he heard the door close behind her. Then he turned and walked stiffly over to his desk, rolled up his sleeves and sat down to work. He worked for several hours, until the music below had stopped and everyone had long gone to bed. Then he leaned back in his chair, kneaded the tired muscles at his neck and stared across at the safe. The door was still open. He picked up the jewellery he had shoved into a corner of his desk, placed it into the case and returned it to the safe. He walked over to the window and looked in the direction of Dune Cottage. *'Catherine!'* he whispered hoarsely, and pressed his brow against the coolness of the glass, his lids closing over the torment in his eyes.

Christmas morning arrived with a blast of sweltering heat, the temperature already climbing past the mid-thirties and it wasn't yet eight o'clock. Catherine sat with a glass of iced tea in her hands watching Jessie unwrap her gifts.

There wasn't much. Catherine had overspent on her birthday but Jessie was thrilled with the little she received, most of it practical: socks, nighties, underwear and the like. But there was one special gift. A shining brand new red two-wheeler bike, a gift from Albert. Betty had added to it with a helmet, basket and bell. The bell had been ringing since six o'clock that morning.

Catherine prepared their breakfast, had a cooling shower and dressed in a pair of loose-fitting shorts and a halter top. The heat was oppressive, the air still, unbelievably still. Jessie rode her bike up and down,

up and down on the veranda. Catherine was relieved
when she finally donned the helmet and went out to
ride it on the driveway.

'Mummy!' Jessie shrieked. 'Come quickly! Come
and see!'

Catherine knew what Jessie wanted. To watch her
ride the bike. A stab of guilt struck her. She shouldn't
be feeling this way, not on Christmas morning. She
felt no joy, no peace. Instead she was listless, entirely
without sparkle. And it wasn't fair to Jessie. She
would have to do better, take a turn on the bike, ring
the bell, laugh, pretend to have fun. Catherine stepped
off the veranda and winced from the fierce glare of
the blazing hot sun. She made her way slowly around
to the back of the cottage to where Jessie was standing
beside the MG, the bike surprisingly forgotten.

'Look, Mummy, look!' Jessie cried excitedly. And
no wonder. Catherine stared and shook her head in
wonder. There were four new tyres on the little red
MG and each one sported an enormous red bow with
sprigs of holly tucked in their centres! The car had
been washed, waxed and polished and gleamed
brightly under the full morning sun. A small white
envelope had been tucked in one of the bows and
poked out invitingly. Catherine's hand trembled as she
reached for it. Tears burned in her eyes as she held
tightly onto it.

'Open it, Mummy. See who it's from.'

But she already knew. She recognised the bold black
scrawl of the hand which had penned her name across
the brilliant white envelope. Her fingers shook as she
drew out the little white card. 'Merry Christmas,
Catherine. Mike.' The words were few but they

meant . . . everything. The letters blurred in front of her eyes.

'It's from Mike,' she told Jessie, and wiped her wet cheeks with the back of her hand.

'Do you want me to take the bows off?' Jessie suggested helpfully.

'No, leave them there. I . . . I like them.'

She loved them! Catherine's heart hammered with joy as she dashed into the cottage and straight to her bedroom. The tyres were much needed and practical but the bows . . . the bows were something else again. A *gesture*! A *romantic* gesture! He wouldn't have gone to so much trouble if he didn't care for her. Perhaps the bows even meant he was sorry for having so misjudged her, a 'Mike-style' apology. He had made her gift special, with not just one bow but four! Catherine smiled as she pulled open her bureau drawer and took out a small framed photograph. She had something for him, too, but after the other evening hadn't ever expected to give it to him.

She gazed down at the photograph in her hands. It was a picture of Dune Cottage at its best taken with Jessie's little camera and enlarged at the photographers. The lawns had just been freshly mowed, and the flowers and shrubs were in full and glorious bloom. She had taken it at sunset when the last rays of the sun splashed against the cottage bathing the tiny structure in a blaze of pink. Standing knee deep in the surf, she had captured the white-tipped waves rolling on to the golden sands, the sands hugging the fringe of green grass and swaying palms. Even the man at the photography shop had admired the photo when she had taken it in to be enlarged and framed.

Catherine had chosen the frame with care. It had to be something dark and masculine but not too dark. It had to fit in with the décor of his study and ... it had to remind him of her. She had finally chosen a smart reddish brown mahogany, almost the exact same shade as her hair, and the soft reddish tonings enhanced the even softer pinks in the photograph. Catherine had gift-wrapped it after their wonderful evening when he had invited them for Christmas dinner but after the incident with the ring ... no, no ... she wasn't going to think about *that* ... but it was after that that she had unwrapped it and placed it face down in her drawer. Now she wrapped it again, lovingly, with shining green paper, and in the exact centre she placed a bow, a white one. He would know what it meant and she pictured his smile when he saw it. Her heart somersaulted in her chest.

She had another shower, shampooed and conditioned her hair, dried and brushed it until her scalp tingled and her hair fell in a smooth, shining bob to her shoulders. She chose her favourite green sundress, the one which always brought out the green flecks in her eyes. She really didn't need make-up, not with her flawless skin which had been tanned to a golden honey colour, but even so she applied a little blusher and touched her long sweeping lashes with just a hint of mascara. Lip gloss came last and when she stepped back to survey the results in the mirror she knew with a burst of joy that she had never looked better. Her whole being seemed to shine, to glow from some inner, mysterious light.

By eleven-thirty they were ready, Jessie dressed in a cool white sun-frock. She wanted to ride her bike and despite the oppressive heat Catherine agreed. If they took the MG, the bows would need to be removed and Catherine didn't want that. She wanted to look at them for as long as possible.

Jessie's wire basket came in handy. Gifts for her mother, Albert, Lucy, Gwen and Mrs Beasley fitted nicely into it. Mike's gift stayed safely in Catherine's hands. The mansion was a beehive of activity when they arrived. Mrs Beasley met them at the door. Catherine immediately handed her her gift. Mrs Beasley stared down at it in surprise then lifted her cold grey eyes to Catherine's face. 'Merry Christmas,' Catherine said softly with a warm smile. Mrs Beasley nodded and looked down at the gift again. When she raised her eyes once more they were no longer cold. And the smile which came to her lips was the first that Catherine had ever seen. 'Merry Christmas,' she said back.

Gwen rushed into the foyer and greeted Catherine and Jessie warmly. They were led into the huge family-room where parents sat watching their youngsters playing with newly acquired gifts. Jessie joined a group on the floor playing with an electric train set. Her mother and Albert sat among the other adults, enjoying the children. Gifts were exchanged, hugs and kisses given out and Catherine's eyes searched the room but Mike . . . and Renata . . . were nowhere to be seen. When a newcomer entered the family room, Catherine's eyes would look up expectantly, then drop in disappointment.

'He's upstairs in his study,' Gwen said softly. 'In fact, we've hardly seen him since the night of the theatre. He's driving himself as if there's no tomorrow on his project in British Columbia. Renata got in a snit and left. She doesn't like playing second fiddle to his work and she's had enough of the kids. They were getting on her nerves.'

Catherine grinned, delighted with this bit of news. She looked down at the precious gift in her hands. She wanted to give it to Mike in private. 'Do you think I could go upstairs to his study? I ... I'd like to ...' She blushed and Gwen chuckled.

'You'd like to give it to Mike in private,' she said for Catherine. 'Sure, go ahead, but I think I should warn you, the boss has been behaving lately like a bear with a thorn in his paw. Jake said at the rate Mike's driving himself, we'll be leaving for Canada much sooner than expected.'

'Leaving?' The word stuck in Catherine's throat.

Gwen eyed her sympathetically. 'He's told you about the ski resort in British Columbia, hasn't he?'

'Yes, but I didn't realise it would be ... soon.' She forced a brightness into her voice. 'I guess you must be getting excited with ... with another adventure to look forward to.'

'Yes, Canada is such a great ...' A loud shriek came from one of the children and Gwen hurriedly raced over to stop a scrimmage before it turned into a full-scale war. Catherine discreetly slipped out of the family room and made her way upstairs. His study door was shut and no sound came from behind its sturdy wooden barrier. Catherine raised her hand to knock and her heart thumped wildly in her chest.

'Who is it?' a deep voice growled from behind, his tone indicating his irritation at being disturbed.

Catherine opened the door cautiously, not making a sound. He was sitting with his back facing her, rolls of blueprints spread across his desk. But he wasn't working on them. Instead he was leaning back in his chair, twirling a slide rule aimlessly in his hands while his feet were propped carelessly on the paper-strewn desktop. Her heart melted at the sight of him.

'It's me,' she answered in a soft, trembling voice, unsure of her reception. 'Catherine.'

His dark head whipped around at the same instant his long legs shot from the desk. He rose slowly from the chair, his deep blue eyes growing darker as his penetrating gaze swept over her as though committing to memory someone special. Someone you knew you wouldn't be seeing again! Her heart cried out in anguish. His eyes were saying *goodbye*!

'May I come in?'

'I think you already are,' he answered with a cold politeness.

Catherine flushed and stepped further inside the room, closing the door behind her. Neither spoke. The silence was suffocating, fuelling the tension between them. His expression was hooded, guarded, as if he really didn't like her, let alone love her! The gift in her hand became suddenly heavy and her hand seemed to sag from the sheer weight of it. She moved further inside the room, her legs feeling as insubstantial as matchsticks as they carried her over to his desk. She put the gift down, near his huge tanned hand, but he didn't pick it up nor did he spare it a glance. His eyes remained on her face, cold and hard. Catherine's heart squeezed painfully in her chest.

'Merry Christmas,' she whispered in a strained voice.

'Merry Christmas,' he returned automatically, his own voice curt, entirely without emotion. Catherine's eyes searched his, desperately seeking any small shred of warmth...and finding none. It was as though he had donned a cold, hard mask to keep her out.

'Thank you for my present,' she managed, thinking her breath was going to be cut off at any moment. 'They were beautiful.'

'Tyres are beautiful?' His voice mocked her.

'When they're wrapped in bows they are.' Her insides were twisted into a painful knot. 'Then...they're very beautiful.'

A dark flush crept across his hard cheeks and for an instant the mask was lifted and she saw torment smoulder briefly in his eyes before the mask dropped once more. It all happened so quickly that Catherine wondered if she had seen it at all.

'I thought they made it more...festive,' he agreed with bored nonchalance, dismissing them as though they had no meaning other than what he had said, a decoration befitting the occasion.

'*I loved them*!' Her voice was a cry of pain.

Mike drew in his breath and held it, keeping some raw emotion in check. Catherine watched the struggle on his face as he warred with something deep and painful within him. She longed to run up to him, to put her arms around him, smooth away the pain in his eyes, touch his hard cheeks, his mouth. She took a tentative step forward, then another and before she knew what she was doing she was running up to him.

She grabbed his shoulders, feeling the strength of his powerful muscles under her trembling hands.

'I love you!' she cried. 'You know I do! Don't block me out. Don't turn me away. I *need* you!' It was a confession straight from her heart.

He grabbed her hands in both of his and held them at her sides, forcing her body away from his and she knew he did it deliberately.

'*Love!*' he snarled, his face darkening with rage. 'What has love brought either of us?'

He smothered whatever reply she might have made by pulling her roughly against him and covering her mouth with the bruising passion of his kiss, his mouth devouring hers with the starving need of what he was so desperately trying to deny them both. He tore his lips from hers and stared down at her with all the violence of an emotion which threatened to rip him apart. 'Love brings death!' he snarled. 'Love brings destruction! You know it and I know it!' He pushed her away from him. 'Now, go,' he commanded and raked a shaking hand through his hair and his body trembled as though from a great weariness. He turned away from her pale face, the shock in her eyes and his eyes caught the gift on his desk. He picked it up, turned it over and Catherine felt sure he would give it back to her without even bothering to open it. But instead, he did open it, and she waited anxiously as he studied it.

'It's a picture of Dune Cottage,' she told him unnecessarily, her voice sounding small in the stillness of the room.

'Very clever!'

Her battered heart stirred and then raced with joy. *He liked it*! She'd known he would. And not only did he like it but he was complimenting her on her expertise as a photographer. Maybe... maybe now... everything would be all right. He hadn't meant what he said. It was just as Gwen had claimed. He had been working too hard, far too hard and...

'But not clever enough!'

Catherine blinked, confused. He placed the framed photo on his desk and looked at her scornfully. 'Obviously you thought I would be so moved by...' he glanced darkly down at the photo '...*this* that I would reconsider having it moved and used by my crews.' He laughed bitterly. 'A very clever little ploy but, as I said, not clever enough!'

Catherine gasped. A ploy? He thought her precious little gift was a... ploy? Anger seeped into her hurt and spread. It made an explosive cocktail.

'You're despicable!' Her face was as white as a sheet and her voice shook. 'I despise you!'

Mike shrugged his broad shoulders. It was almost as though he had expected her to say something like that, had deliberately egged her into it.

'A moment ago you said you loved me,' he heartlessly reminded her. His blue-black eyes coldly mocked her. 'Love sure doesn't last long these days!'

He strolled over to the door and opened it. 'Now, if you will excuse me, I'd like to get ready for dinner.'

Dismissed! She was being dismissed. Catherine walked with as much dignity as she could muster under the circumstances, and with head held high, passed him without looking at him, straight out the door.

She heard it close behind her like he was closing her out of his heart. Tears stung her eyes and she viciously swiped at them. How could she have been so stupid as to think the bows had meant something? How could she have been so naïve as to think he would be charmed and enchanted by a picture of Dune Cottage? She was so *stupid*! So *naïve*!

Dinner was a nightmare. A nightmare in a heavenly setting. The enormous dining table had been laid with a sparkling white linen cloth with a huge potted poinsettia in its centre, scarlet and green against the white. Wedgwood, crystal and silver sparkled and gleamed under the dozens of tiny lights from the elaborate chandelier above the table. In the far corner of the dining-room stood a massive Christmas tree, towering up and almost touching the ceiling. The tree had been decorated with gold, red and green bells and it was ablaze with hundreds of sparkling lights.

Mike sat at the head of the table, a king presiding over his courtiers. He had changed into navy trousers and a royal blue shirt, the colour exactly matching his eyes. He had shaved and showered and his black hair was still slightly damp at the edges. Catherine was certain she had never seen him look so handsome.

The meal was superb, turkey with all the trimmings. The conversation focused entirely on their forthcoming project. Catherine listened and her heart grew lonelier with each word. Several times she felt Mike's eyes on her but whenever she looked quickly up, heart hammering, it was only to find she had been mistaken. She hardly uttered a word throughout the entire meal. There was nothing for her to say. She looked around at the engineers, the architects, the geologists. She looked at Gwen and the other women, busily outlining their plans for keeping the children occupied and talking about their schooling. And often she looked at Mike, their leader and employer, and she couldn't help but wonder if he wasn't deliberately keeping the talk focused on the project in another attempt to shut her out. When the dessert of plum pudding smothered in a white brandy sauce was finally served and eaten, Catherine made her escape. The women were busy with their children, putting the younger ones down for naps. The men had gone out to the veranda to continue their discussion, and she left Jessie to play with the older children and to pass around the peppermint canes she had brought them for a special treat. No one even seemed to notice she was going... it was as if they had already departed on their great adventure.

Despite the heat she raced through the wood, following the path to the cottage. Once inside, she pulled off her dress and under garments and slipped into her bikini. But she had no intention of going into the surf. She pulled shorts and a shirt over her bikini, slipped her feet into a pair of sandals, grabbed a wide-brimmed straw hat and hurried out the door. She was heading for her own special place, the rock pools hidden in its ferny jungle and surrounded by the rich green carpet of moss. There she could suffer in peace, with some sort of dignity, and she would try to get over the thought of never seeing Mike again, for she knew that was what he wanted, what he planned. He would leave for British Columbia and, apart from a few lightning trips back to Australia, he would be gone for at least a year.

And during that year he would forget all about her. This she knew. This was his plan. And the thought of it was unbearable. Totally.

CHAPTER TWELVE

CATHERINE stumbled along the narrow overgrown path, oblivious to the blinding heat which soaked her shirt, her hair, and brought the blood pounding to her cheeks. Several times she tripped and almost fell, but she was hardly aware of this. Her mission was to get to the pools and the sooner the better. Her heart was bursting with grief but she refused to allow herself to think of anything until she was surrounded in total peace and tranquillity. And then, only then, would she release the pent-up emotions which were ripping her apart.

A jagged root caught her sandal and she fell heavily to the scorched ground. She lay, stunned, for several seconds, and it was only after a deep sob tore from her throat was she able to pull herself up and continue her journey. She couldn't give in here, not here, where it wasn't peaceful, or cool, or her own special place. When at last she heard the sound of rushing water, she increased her speed despite the heat and the fact she was on the brink of exhaustion. She was almost there . . . she could smell the water . . . the air was already cooler . . . there was music . . .

Music! Catherine stopped short. Music? How could there be *music*? She removed her hat and ran her fingers through her thick, damp tresses. It was all right. She was tired, that was all. Sleep hadn't come easily the past few nights and this heat, this unbearable heat was responsible for making her hear things that couldn't possibly be there. She replaced her straw hat and trudged on, following the sound of the cascading water and trying to ignore the fact that the music was getting louder.

She stopped behind the towering fringe of ferns and dropped to her knees. There was no point in denying any longer that someone was there, swimming in her pool, robbing her of a chance to explore her desolate heart, ease her aching pain. Catherine parted the ferns just wide enough to see who it was, and to hope they would soon be on their way. Her eyes rounded in incredulous disbelief and a startled gasp tore from her throat.

Mike!

Her hands trembled on the ferns and then she dropped them quickly. Her mind whirled. What was he doing here? She had seen him go out to the veranda with the other men. How had he found this place? She had always meant to tell him about it, take him here, show him this place which was *her* place, share it with him, *give* it to him! And now here he was, enjoying it on his own, and she felt cheated, robbed and her despair grew and she felt suffocated by it.

But she had to look again, look at her love. She parted the ferns once more to watch him in secret. His hair was flattened against his head, wet, black and sleek. He cut through the crystal-clear water with long, powerful strokes, the rippling muscles of his tanned shoulders glistening under the green-tinted sun. He ploughed to the opposite end of the pool, ducked under and ploughed back again. The water became a churning mass of frenzied foam as he beat at it with

the powerful strokes of his legs and the grasping reach
of his arms. It was an awesome sight and despite the
heat, Catherine shivered. She knew what Mike was
doing. He was chasing away the devils which gripped
his soul, and it made her think maybe he was suffering too just as she was, and she thought how crazy
it was, both of them suffering, both of them hurting
because he was ... afraid of love!

The churning stopped but she could see by the set
of his face that he wasn't at peace. He leaned with
his back against the velvet mossy edge of the rock
pool, arms spread out on either side, his breathing
deep, his eyes fixed on something she knew he wasn't
really seeing. Beside him were trousers and shirt, sun-
glasses and transistor radio. He looked at the radio
and abruptly switched it off, as though the soft, al-
luring music was suddenly irritating. Catherine remained crouched in her hiding position, instinct telling
her he would be leaving soon, now. She didn't want
him to go. She wanted to be able to watch him forever.
But even as she was thinking this, he levered himself
out of the pool with his arms in one graceful fluid
movement.

And stood in front of her totally naked! Silky black
hair curled wetly across his chest and the strong brown
columns of his legs stood slightly apart, feet pressed
into the spongy green moss. He raised his arms, fingers
pointed upwards to shake the water from his hair, and
his eyes caught something behind the ferns. His deep
blue eyes narrowed and Catherine shrank back. But
it was too late. Those eyes, those all seeing eyes, had
already spotted her. One huge hand reached between
the thick green ferns and closed itself around her

shoulder. He dragged her out and she stood in front
of him, cheeks scarlet, eyes lowered, fixed on the small
pools of water forming around his feet. He muttered
a curse as he remembered his state of undress, released her and grabbed his trousers, whipped them
on, eyes blazing.

'How long have you been hiding there, spying on
me?' he demanded harshly.

'Not long,' she answered truthfully and truth gave
way to defiance as she added heatedly. 'And I wasn't
spying!'

'Of course you weren't! How foolish of me to think
you were!' His spiky black lashes did nothing to
conceal the cold rage in the pearly midnight blue of
his eyes. 'And I suppose you didn't follow me up here
either?'

'I didn't.' She glowered up at him. 'I often come
up here.'

He seemed surprised by this and she realised he must
have considered this his own special place just as she
had. Again she was struck by the absurdity of it all.
They could have been enjoying it together.

'Well, I'm here now,' he needlessly pointed out.
'And I wish to be alone.'

'The whole of your life?' she flared angrily,
hurtfully.

His eyes narrowed. 'What's that supposed to
mean?'

'You know damn well,' she thundered. 'Gwen has
told me how hard you've been working to speed up
your departure for Canada. It's to get away from me,
isn't it? Because you're *afraid* of me and . . .'

A loud snort filled the still air. 'Afraid of you, Catherine? Don't be...'

She stamped her foot. 'Let me *finish*!' Green daggers shot from her eyes as she glared up at him. 'You're a rich and powerful man, Michael Donahue, but you're also a coward!'

Mike stared down at her in open-mouthed astonishment. When he opened his mouth to speak again, Catherine hurried on. Nothing was going to keep her from saying what had to be said, what she needed to say if she was ever going to get on with her life after he had gone. 'Your first marriage failed. *So what*? It shouldn't mean you should never try again. What would have happened if your first business venture had failed? Would you have thrown in the towel? I think *not*! You would have tried harder, done better, made sure you never made the same mistake again.'

'That's exactly what I am doing,' Mike stated between gritted teeth. 'Making sure I never make the same mistake again!' He dragged a hand roughly through his wet hair. 'You've said enough, Catherine. I'd... appreciate it if you would go now.'

The colour drained from her face and in her eyes was all the hurt and despair which flooded up from her heart. 'You're a fool, Mike,' she whispered brokenly. 'I love you but I'm going to try my hardest to get over you.' Her voice broke. 'And I will... because you don't deserve me!' She started to turn away, to follow the narrow, overgrown track back to the cottage, but she whirled back, angry tears burning brightly in her eyes. How dare he order her away. She had no intention of meekly doing his bidding.

'No!' she cried. 'I *won't* go! I ... I came for a swim and a swim I shall have.' She yanked off her hat and flung it to the ground. She dived neatly into the cold, clear pool, swam smoothly to the opposite side, climbed on to the soft spongy moss, removed her shirt and shorts ... and then casually removed her bikini!

She did it slowly, seductively, her back facing him, her fingers finding the clasp of her yellow bikini top, unfastening it and allowing it to trail down her body to the ground. Then she kicked it away with the toe of her foot. She wriggled out of the bottoms, slipping one long slender leg out at a time, her hands trailing lightly over their smoothness as she did so. Her rich mane of chestnut-coloured hair tumbled across her shoulders and she lifted it with her hands, held it there for several seconds in a seductive pose, before she allowed it to fall to the rounded curves of her shoulders.

Catherine felt intoxicated by her boldness. Her body burned with a raw, sensuous awareness, every pulsating nerve alerted to the eyes she knew watched from the other side of the pool. She sank to the moss-covered ground, her back arched gracefully, eyes closed, face lifted in profile to the dappled sun.

Droplets of water trickled from her hair and rolled down her spine. She gave a convulsive little shiver as though they were *his* fingers teasing her delicate skin. She heard the quiet splash he made as he dived into the pool and his almost silent strokes as he covered the short distance separating them. She felt the sudden coolness of his shadow as he stood over her. Her breath quickened and she opened her eyes.

His eyes gleamed down at her, dark and dangerous. Her mouth went completely dry when his hands went to the waistband of his trousers and undid the buckle of his belt and then very slowly the zipper of his trousers. The material clung wetly to the hard contours of his muscular thighs. His eyes held hers in a paralysing grip as he eased the trousers over narrow hips and hard buttocks. Then he stood before her, proud and majestic, and she knew she would soon be conquered and knew too that this was what she wanted.

Her fingers trembled as she longed to touch him, trace the outline of those hard muscles, feel the texture of his skin and hair. Her drugged eyes travelled up his powerful height and came to rest on his face. His dark head was thrown slightly back and a fierce light burned in his eyes. The look was as ancient as the beginning of time and so was her response. He held out his hands and she took them and he raised her up to meet him.

His eyes moved over her, drinking in her beauty, resting on the dark burnished red-brown of her hair, her ripe uptilted breasts.

'You're sensational,' he said gruffly, his voice thickened with desire. 'You've got the body of a seductress, the face of an angel.' He raised his hands to touch her hair, his fingers moving it away from her face, silken strands clinging to his roughened skin.

His hands moved down her neck and across her shoulders and she could feel the tension burning in them, fanning the already blazing fires deep within her body.

He pulled her against him, his mouth burning on hers, his lips hard and hot against her neck, her shoulders, her breasts. Waves of red-hot currents rippled through her body, crashed into the pit of her stomach. Mike picked her up and laid her down on the soft green carpet of moss. His eyes were black with passion as he leaned over her, his mouth like liquid flames as he explored her writhing body.

Afterwards they lay in each other's arms, panting, bodies soaked in sweat, eyes glazed and cheeks flushed. It was a long time before either stirred and when they did, and Mike raised himself on his elbows to look into her eyes, each knew neither had ever experienced anything like it before. And all they could do at that very moment was to look into each other's eyes and smile.

He rolled off her and lay on his back, his chest still heaving, one arm across his eyes to shade them from the dappled sun filtering through the towering ferns. Catherine rolled on to her side and propped herself up on her elbow and looked lovingly down at him. His lips were slightly parted and she could see the white gleam of his teeth against his darkened skin. He removed his arm and gazed up at her, his eyes still dark and deep with the aftermath of their passion. His hand reached out and he touched her firm breast, felt the smoothness of its rounded shape. He rubbed his thumb lightly over it and smiled when it became aroused. 'Come closer,' he growled, and Catherine did. The tip of her breast brushed against his lips and he touched it with his tongue and drew it into his mouth, his teeth nibbling on it gently. Catherine trembled and felt the flames start again in her stomach, deep and low. With his mouth still on her breast, Mike rolled her on to her back and he began to make love to her all over again, his hands at first gentle, but his caresses becoming more urgent as she responded with a burning aching desire and their cries once more shattered the sweet stillness of the pools until finally they were at rest.

Catherine sat still and watched him. She felt certain he was asleep. His eyes were closed and his face was totally at peace. She felt peaceful too, cleansed, and she marvelled at the feeling. She knew he loved her! His hands, his mouth, his body had told her so. Love couldn't be hidden...but...it could be denied. She knew nothing would be the same between them again. What would he do now, she couldn't help but wonder. Say goodbye to her? Could he really do that? Now? Her eyes trailed lovingly, achingly, admiringly down the entire length of his body. He had possessed her, made her his, claimed her—oh, how he had claimed her!

But she knew how hard he had fought against loving her. It all seemed so silly now. His suspicions about her being at Dune Cottage and his warning not to become too comfortable...the watch...the ring. But his eyes...those deep blue eyes... She smiled and looked down at the long spiky lashes resting against his hard cheeks. His eyes had always managed to tell her that his heart was calling out to her. His words had hurt, though...sometimes deeply...but now she knew they had merely been weapons...weapons to defend himself against his growing love. Catherine sighed happily and pulled her knees up to her chin and wrapped her slender arms around her legs. Why did such a wonderful emotion have to be so complicated?

Mike sat up beside her, stood and stretched. She watched him with a blinding love in her eyes.

'I thought you were asleep,' she said softly, and rose to her feet.

'No, just resting.' He didn't look at her and his voice was curt. He reached for his trousers, gave them a shake and started to slip into them. He glanced at his watch. 'Hell!'

'Is it very late?' she asked, a tremble in her voice and the light gradually fading from her eyes.

'Late enough.' He zipped his trousers and fastened the buckle. 'Get dressed, Catherine. You will get wet but it can't be avoided. The pool is too deep to walk across.' He picked up her clothes and handed them to her. Her fingers felt lifeless as she accepted them. He was behaving like a stranger, a cold, unloving stranger.

'Thanks,' she mumbled, and turned her back to him in a foolish gesture of modesty to dress into her damp shorts and shirt. She stuffed her bikini into one of her pockets. When she turned he was standing at the edge of the pool, ready to dive in but politely waiting for her, courteous to the end. And she knew it was the end. She had given him everything she had and given it willingly. She had taken her heart and placed it in his hands. He had wrung it dry and given it back. She walked stiffly to the edge of the pool. Her throat ached. She couldn't swallow.

'You...shouldn't have given me the bows,' she whispered tragically. 'It...it would have been so much...easier...if you hadn't.'

His hand snaked out and caught her wrist, his iron grip hurting her but she hardly noticed. She was beyond feeling. Hurt had made her numb. 'I warned you, Catherine,' he said, his voice taut, gravelled, checking an emotion not fully conquered. 'Love brings nothing but...'

She wrenched her hand free. 'I know. You told me. I don't want to hear it again. I only want you to know, you're wrong.' The lump in her throat threatened to strangle her and she tried desperately to swallow it. 'Love doesn't bring death and destruction. It brings truth and beauty and hope. Love gave me Jessie and there will always be a special place in my heart for her father.' Tears brimmed in her eyes. 'Your marriage broke down but it gave you Lucy. Love...should be rewarded...not *blamed*!'

Catherine dived into the pool and scrambled out the other side. Water coursed down from her hair and blended with her tears. She heard Mike shouting behind her but she didn't turn, nor did she stop to pick up her hat or grab her sandals. She parted the ferns and raced blindly down the narrow and steep path.

She knew what she must do. *Leave*! Leave the cottage and never come back. She should have done it ages ago, should have done it that very first night when he had accused her so unjustly. Perhaps then she wouldn't be feeling this way now, broken and shattered. There wasn't much to pack, just their clothes, books and a few toys. They had come with little and they would leave...

Catherine smelt the smoke as soon as she left the tangled forest of ferns. She saw it rising in the sky, thick and yellow. Fear squeezed her aching heart. She raced down the remaining bit of track and on to the cleared land of the estate. The smoke was billowing above Dune Cottage.

Dune Cottage was on fire!

CHAPTER THIRTEEN

THE cottage was a blazing inferno. Leaves rose from the fiery compost heap, each one a burning torch, spinning in the still air and fluttering like crazy things onto the crackling roof. Catherine screamed and raced towards the beloved little structure, frantically searching for the garden hose in the thick acrid smoke. The ferocious heat struck and forced her back. In the distance she could hear the wail of a fire engine but it would arrive *too late*!

Sobbing, she found the hose and, shielding her face with her arm, edged towards the scorching heat. Behind her, someone roared a name but she barely heard it or recognised it to be her name. The thin squirt of the water from the hose was a mockery and she forced herself closer still . . . she *must* get closer!

Strong arms grabbed her. The hose was ripped from her hands and flung away. She stared into Mike's white face and she was filled with rage. She punched his arms and chest, kicked his shins and screamed at him to let her go. He picked her up and ran with her to the fringe of the wood. People were running towards them . . . from the mansion. They had come to watch her cottage *burn*! They stood there, gaping at the fire, doing *nothing* to help, to *save* it. She screamed again at Mike to let her go and pounded viciously at his chest, pulled at his hair but he only held more tightly onto her. Suddenly she felt herself being flung into someone else's arms, Jake's, and Mike was ordering him to hold on to her, not to let her go. Infuriated, Catherine struggled to be released as her wild eyes followed Mike's retreating back. He was rushing over to Albert. Betty was trying to hold him up, struggling with his limp body. Catherine became still when Mike lowered his father's body gently to the ground. He leaned over him, pressed his ear to his father's chest. Betty's face was white with anguish as Mike worked frantically on his father, his hands rising and falling on his chest.

Jake released her. Gwen rounded up the children and the others and they started slowly back to the mansion. Jake walked over to Mike and laid his hand on Mike's shoulder. The fire truck arrived, hoses unreeled. But it was all over. The cottage was a bed of red embers; the compost heap a bed of smouldering ashes. Mike picked up the frail, still body and carried him in his arms back to the mansion. Betty followed, her head bowed in grief. Jake's arm was around Betty's shoulders, comforting her, his expression bleak. The firemen reeled up their hoses. Catherine heard them say the fire was caused by the compost heap. Spontaneous combustion, they said. The truck drove away. There was no one left. Catherine was alone. All alone.

She turned stiffly and clawed her way up to the dunes. It was almost dark. The first stars were already out. She stood at the edge and stared blindly out to sea. Tears streamed silently down her frozen cheeks.

The sky grew darker, the stars brighter. Still she stood there, a tragic figure frozen in grief, listening to the voice which haunted her . . . had warned her.

Love brings only death and destruction!

Albert was dead. *Death*!

The cottage was destroyed. *Destruction*!

If only she had *listened* to him. He had been *right*! Her love had driven her to the rock pools. If she hadn't gone she would have been here to put out the fire in the compost heap. It would have taken only a few minutes, forgotten a few minutes later. Albert, sweet, wonderful Albert, would still be alive, the cottage still standing. Mike and her mother wouldn't be suffering now; the children and the others wouldn't have had to witness the horror they had.

It was *her* fault! *She* had killed the frail old gentleman. *She* had destroyed the cottage, broken everyone's hearts. Her legs finally gave way beneath her and she sank slowly to the sand. Her body convulsed with grief, shook with her agony. She would never forget the pain in Mike's eyes as he picked up his father's body... or the grief in her mother's as she touched the snow-white head. Her moans filled the still night air. She wanted to die. She didn't deserve to live. She didn't deserve anything, not even her precious Jessie.

'Catherine!'

She heard his voice and she stiffened. She couldn't face him. Not *now*. Not *yet*. Her tragic eyes searched the darkness, wildly searching for a means of escape... to hide from the horrible grief and blame she knew would be in his eyes. She rose to her hands and knees, a small wounded animal, scurrying away from the hunter.

'Catherine!' he said again, his voice filled with a tragic emotion which further tore at her heart. She

stopped in her tracks, head lowered to hide her
grieving shame. Mike knelt beside her and she dared
a look, a small peeping glance to measure his hurt,
his anger, his condemnation. But there was only one
emotion on the darkly handsome features. *Sorrow*!
It ripped her up... split her in half.

'I killed him!' she screamed hysterically. 'I killed
your *father*!'

There, she'd said it, told him what she had done.
She waited, coiled like a spring, waiting for his reaction, bracing herself for the hatred and revulsion
she knew would come. But there was no hatred, no
revulsion, only a deep weariness in his eyes. He hadn't
understood! she thought wildly. '*Albert's dead*! I
killed him!' She jumped to her feet and flung her arm
wildly in the direction of the burnt out shell of the
cottage. 'I did that, *too*! I *destroyed* your *cottage*!
You won't be able to use it now as a...'

Mike had risen when she had. He grabbed her arm.
'Catherine, stop it! *Listen* to me...'

'But I didn't *listen* to you!' she cried shrilly. 'I
should have... but I didn't and...'

Her head snapped back as he struck her hard across
the cheek, red streaks appearing almost immediately
across the cold marble paleness of her face. She sagged
and crumpled against him and he gathered her into
his arms and she felt the strong hammering beat of
his heart against her cheek.

'Albert's fine,' he told her straight away. 'It was
touch and go for a while but my father's as strong as
an ox. He's in hospital... your mother is with
him... she won't leave his side... but he's going to
be fine, just fine.' He held her slightly away from him

to make certain she understood. Catherine stared up at him, her eyes haunted shadows in her small white face.

'He didn't die?' she asked and her voice sounded hollow like coming from a ghost.

'He didn't die,' Mike quietly assured her and his arms trembled as he tried to gather her close again to warm her against his heart. But Catherine's frozen body stiffened and she pulled herself away.

'The cottage is gone,' she said because it was important to remind him of what she was certain he must have forgotten. 'My compost heap caught fire. I heard the firemen talking. They said the burning leaves ignited the curtains. It wouldn't have happened if I'd been here or if I hadn't left the windows open.'

'Thank God you weren't here!' His voice was raw, choked with emotion. 'You might have been badly hurt.' He reached out a hand to touch her hair but she stepped quickly back and his eyes darkened even more. 'It's been so hot. The compost heap literally exploded. The cottage was old, the wood dry. Nothing could have saved it. You mustn't blame yourself for any of this.'

She didn't pay any attention. She *knew* it was her fault. 'Your work crews won't have a lunch mess now,' she said, 'or an office.' She waited and watched but she somehow felt the sorrow in his eyes wasn't because his crews were going to miss out.

He grabbed her shoulders and once more she stiffened, her face pale in the moonlight. 'I don't give a *damn* about the cottage!' he told her, his voice choked with a raw emotion. 'I won't be building a resort here!'

Her eyes widened and flooded with a new guilt. 'Because of what I've done?' she whispered.

Mike shook his head and his huge hands trembled on her arms but he kept her at a distance, not wanting to upset her anymore than she already was. 'Yes,' he cried hoarsely, his eyes burning pools in his haggard face. 'Because you love this place and because of all the work you did to make it so charming and beautiful. I decided a while back not to build, at least not here. There's some land further up the coast...I've started negotiations...I'll build there...'

Fresh pain filled his eyes as she wrenched herself free of his hands and turned her back on him to gaze down to where the cottage had once stood, where she and Jessie had been so happy, where they'd spent their first ever holiday.

And Mike hadn't given a damn about the place. That was what he'd said. Apart from herself and Jessie, her mother and Albert, no one would miss it. She knew she would have left it, had planned to do so, but that was only because her love for Mike had made it impossible for her to stay. Now, everything was gone. Everything she and Jessie owned had been destroyed. Their clothes, books, toys, money, all gone. Her car keys had been in her purse. They couldn't even drive away. The little bit of money, enough to keep them until she started working and received her first pay, was no more. She stared bleakly down at the smouldering remains.

Mike came up behind her. He touched her shoulder. She was as stiff as a board. He turned her gently around. She squeezed her eyes shut so she wouldn't have to look at him. He cupped her chin in his hand

and lifted her face. 'Open your eyes, Catherine,' he said softly. She pretended not to hear. If she looked at him, even a glimpse, she knew she would be finished. And she couldn't afford to be finished. She had her child to consider, a future to face and she didn't know how she was going to do it but knew she must...somehow, she must.

His fingers stroked her eyelids and wiped away the tears streaming down her cheeks. 'I've hurt you, Catherine,' he said, his voice a hoarse whisper and she heard his pain. Her eyes opened, just a little. But it was enough to see the suffering in his face. 'And I hurt you deliberately because I loved you so much!'

Catherine's eyes flew open, wide and staring and disbelieving. She felt her heart slowly coming to life in her chest.

'You...you loved me?'

'I'll always love you!' he cried fiercely. 'I fell in love with you the night you danced on the dunes. It was as if you had danced straight into my heart and no matter what I did, the more I said to try and get you out, the more I wanted, needed for you to stay.'

Catherine's numbed brain spun back to that first night when she had felt so deliriously happy, when she had danced....*naked*! Colour finally rose to her pale cheeks. 'You *saw* me?'

'I saw you and I fell in love with you. You danced so freely, moved so beautifully.' His eyes burned with the intensity of his feelings. 'And then when I saw you on the veranda...the way you looked at me...the way you made me feel, well, that's when I realised I had to do everything in my power to get rid of you.'

'But *why*?'

'Why?' His voice became bitter. 'Because after Gail, with all the hurt and trouble she caused, I vowed I would never marry again.'

'I...I vowed I would never remarry after my husband died. I didn't want to be hurt like that again, but...but you hurt me far more.'

And the hurt he had caused her rose in his eyes for her to see and feel and understand. She reached out her hand and touched his hard cheek. A mighty tremble ripped through his body and she heard his cry of anguish.

'If only you will let me, if only you will give me a chance, I swear I'll spend the rest of my life making you happy, making sure you will never be hurt again.' He clasped her hands in his, holding on to them tightly, and she saw the naked plea in his eyes, but, more than that, she saw and heard his love and she was overwhelmed with her emotions. *He loved her*! He had loved her from the *beginning*!

'Would you have gone to Canada...' she swallowed hard '...without me?'

'No!' He shook his dark head. 'But you were right when you said I was working hard to leave sooner. I was losing the battle...I was losing control. I felt like breaking Curtis in half when you dated him. I was even jealous of the watch my father gave you.' He dragged his hand through his hair as though he couldn't quite believe all the things he had done, thought and felt. 'But when you said you were going to forget me, well, that was when I knew I could never forget you. When you climbed out of the pool I called after you. I wanted to tell you how I felt and beg your forgiveness.' He framed her face in his huge hands

and gazed lovingly down at her. 'So, I'm asking you
now.' He kissed the tip of her nose. 'Will you forgive
me, darling? Enough to marry me?'

Her face was soft and beautiful in the moonlight
and her eyes shone from the reflected light, brimming
with all the love she felt for this man. 'Oh, Mike,' she
whispered lovingly. 'I love you so much I could burst
from the feeling.' She wrapped her arms around his
waist and placed her cheek against his heart, the heart
which had been hers from the beginning and which
she would look after and love and cherish until the
end.

'And you'll marry me?' he murmured huskily
against her ear.

Catherine smiled, a deliriously happy smile. 'I'll
marry you!'

His arms closed around her as he held her tightly
against him. There, under the moonlight, they began
to sway. Sway to the rhythm of their heartbeats and
the magic of their love. The stars twinkled above them
and the waves rolled against the banks of the majestic
dunes. And Mike held firmly on to his love, his eyes
closed above her sweet smelling hair, his body moving
with hers in perfect tune to his little dune dancer!

Catherine dismissed her class. 'See you after the
Christmas holidays,' she cheerfully called after them
as they rushed out to the corridor. She got up from
her desk and walked across the bare wooden floor to
the window. Her face broke out in a grin. Gwen was
doing her best to keep a snowball game from becoming a snowball brawl. She spotted Jessie and Lucy
in the midst of it, their faces rosy, their bright red

scarves trailing behind them, their navy blue snow-suits not hampering them a bit as they charged a fort.

It had been almost a year now since the cottage had burnt to the ground and Mike had confessed his love. Mike had drawn up plans for a new cottage and Albert and Betty had supervised its construction. It had everything in it they wanted, and Betty's letters to Catherine had told her the enjoyment they'd received from it. Sometimes, Betty had confessed, they even spent the odd night there! Catherine knew they longed to live in the cottage and perhaps some day they would, when Albert no longer needed the special equipment installed at the mansion to maintain his health.

Albert had bought Betty a brand new Mercedes to drive them around the countryside and quite often Mrs Beasley joined them, past hostilities long forgotten. Mike had purchased the coastal property he had been negotiating for and was already drawing up plans for his new resort. Catherine delighted in offering bits and pieces of advice and loved to sit and watch him draw and marvel at his brilliance.

As Catherine gazed out the window, soft thick flurries of snow began hitting the pane. She had never experienced a white Christmas before and was certainly looking forward to this one. They would return to Australia in time for New Year and to visit the family. And to celebrate their first wedding anniversary! She hadn't thought it possible to love her man any more than the day she had said, 'I do!' but her love had simply grown and grown.

The flurries grew bigger and thicker and she became anxious. While the other men had returned from the

construction site almost an hour ago, Mike hadn't.
He always remained after everyone else had left to
make certain everything was secure with his massive
ski project. Her eyes were fixed on the snow-packed
trail leading into the rugged white-capped mountains
and disappearing between the green timber-tops.
When she saw the snowmobile hurtling down the trail,
a brilliant smile replaced her anxiety. She ran to get
her parka and was there to meet him when he pulled
up to the schoolhouse door.

His thick black hair was flecked with snow, his
rough cheeks reddened by the wind, and his blue eyes
sparkled at the sight of her. He held out his arm and
helped her on to the seat behind him. Catherine put
her arms around his waist and snuggled into the
warmth of his neck. The two little girls broke free
from their group and raced up to them. They too
jumped on to the snowmobile for a fun ride up to
their cheery log bungalow which had been home for
almost a year.

And once inside Catherine knew what would
happen. Mike would light a fire in the huge hearth
while Catherine plugged in the kettle. Jessie and Lucy
would switch on the Christmas tree lights and gaze
excitedly at the gifts beneath the tree. She would carry
the tea and the little shortcakes into the lounge and
place them on the rugged pine coffee-table in front
of the hearth. And only then would she permit herself
to look at the gifts.

The ones with the big red bows were for her. She
would smile, and Mike would see that smile, and when
she looked at him, her eyes would tell him she had
known all along what those bows had meant!

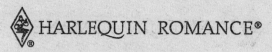

HARLEQUIN ROMANCE®

brings you

More Romances Celebrating Love, Families and Children!

Harlequin Romance #3362

THE BABY BUSINESS

by

Rebecca Winters

If you love babies—this book is for you!

When hotel nanny Rachel Ellis searches for her lost
brother, she meets his boss—the dashing and gorgeous
Vincente de Raino. She is unprepared for her strong
attraction to him, but even more unprepared to be left
holding the baby—his adorable baby niece, Luisa, who
makes her long for a baby of her own!

Available in May wherever Harlequin Books are sold.

KIDS12

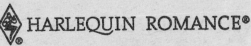

HARLEQUIN ROMANCE®

brings you

Harlequin Romance #3361, *Mail-Order Bridegroom*,
in our Sealed with a Kiss series next month is by one of
our most popular authors, **Day Leclaire.**

Leah Hampton needs a husband for her ranch
to survive—a strictly no-nonsense business arrangement.
Advertising for one in the local newspaper makes good
sense, but she finds to her horror a reply from none other
than Hunter Pryde, the man she had been in love with
eight years before!

Is her fate sealed with one kiss? Or can she resist falling
in love with him all over again?

In the coming months, look for these exciting
Sealed with a Kiss stories:

Harlequin Romance #3366
P.S. I Love You by Valerie Parv in June

Harlequin Romance #3369
Wanted: Wife and Mother by Barbara McMahon in July

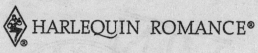

HARLEQUIN ROMANCE®

celebrates

FAMILY TIES!

**Join us in June for our brand-new miniseries—
Family Ties!**

Family... What does it bring to mind? The trials and
pleasures of children and grandchildren, loving parents
and close bonds with brothers and sisters—that special
joy a close family can bring. Whatever meaning it has for
you, we know you'll enjoy these heartwarming love stories
in which we celebrate family—and in which you can
meet some fascinating members of our
heroes' and heroines' families.

The first title to look out for is...
Simply the Best
by Catherine Spencer

followed by...

Make Believe Marriage
by Renee Roszel in July

FT-G-R

Fifty red-blooded, white-hot, true-blue hunks
from every State in the Union!

Look for MEN MADE IN AMERICA! Written by some
of our most popular authors, these stories feature some
of the strongest, sexiest men, each from a different state
in the union!

Two titles available every month at your favorite
retail outlet.

In April, look for:

FOR THE LOVE OF MIKE
by Candace Schuler (Texas)
THE DEVLIN DARE
by Cathy Thacker (Virginia)

In May, look for:

A TIME AND A SEASON
by Curtiss Ann Matlock (Oklahoma)
SPECIAL TOUCHES
by Sharon Brondos (Wyoming)

You won't be able to resist MEN MADE IN AMERICA!

Harlequin invites you to the most
romantic wedding of the season.

Rope the cowboy of your dreams in
Marry Me, Cowboy!

A collection of 4 brand-new stories,
celebrating weddings, written by:

New York Times bestselling author

JANET DAILEY

and favorite authors

Margaret Way
Anne McAllister
Susan Fox

Be sure not to miss Marry Me, Cowboy!
coming this April

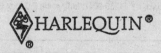HARLEQUIN®

HARLEQUIN®

Don't miss these Harlequin favorites by some of our most
distinguished authors!
And now, you can receive a discount by ordering two or more titles!

HT #25607	PLAIN JANE'S MAN by Kristine Rolofson	$2.99 U.S./$3.50 CAN.	☐
HT #25616	THE BOUNTY HUNTER		
	by Vicki Lewis Thompson	$2.99 U.S./$3.50 CAN.	☐
HP #11674	THE CRUELLEST LIE by Susan Napier	$2.99 U.S./$3.50 CAN.	☐
HP #11699	ISLAND ENCHANTMENT by Robyn Donald	$2.99 U.S./$3.50 CAN.	☐
HR #03268	THE BAD PENNY by Susan Fox	$2.99	☐
HR #03303	BABY MAKES THREE by Emma Goldrick	$2.99	☐
HS #70570	REUNITED by Evelyn A. Crowe	$3.50	☐
HS #70611	ALESSANDRA & THE ARCHANGEL		
	by Judith Arnold	$3.50 U.S./$3.99 CAN.	☐
HI #22291	CRIMSON NIGHTMARE		
	by Patricia Rosemoor	$2.99 U.S./$3.50 CAN.	☐
HAR #16549	THE WEDDING GAMBLE by Muriel Jensen	$3.50 U.S./$3.99 CAN.	☐
HAR #16558	QUINN'S WAY by Rebecca Flanders	$3.50 U.S./$3.99 CAN.	☐
HH #28802	COUNTERFEIT LAIRD by Erin Yorke	$3.99	☐
HH #28824	A WARRIOR'S WAY by Margaret Moore	$3.99 U.S./$4.50 CAN.	☐

(limited quantities available on certain titles)

	AMOUNT	$
DEDUCT:	10% DISCOUNT FOR 2+ BOOKS	$
ADD:	POSTAGE & HANDLING	$
	($1.00 for one book, 50¢ for each additional)	
	APPLICABLE TAXES*	$_____
	TOTAL PAYABLE	$_____
	(check or money order—please do not send cash)	

To order, complete this form and send it, along with a check or money order for the
total above, payable to Harlequin Books, to: **In the U.S.:** 3010 Walden Avenue,
P.O. Box 9047, Buffalo, NY 14269-9047; **In Canada:** P.O. Box 613, Fort Erie, Ontario,
L2A 5X3.

Name:_____

Address:_____ City:_____

State/Prov.:_____ Zip/Postal Code:_____

*New York residents remit applicable sales taxes.
 Canadian residents remit applicable GST and provincial taxes.   HBACK-AJ2